belonging with her best friend

a sweet romantic comedy

kristin canary

To Dad,
for modeling what true love looks like

one

· · ·

I CAN THINK of a thousand things I would rather endure than the moment I'm living in right now.

Sky diving (that seems obvious). Going on *The Amazing Race* (how stressful does that show look?). Getting thrown up on by all thirty of my kindergarten students—at once.

Telling my best friend, Eric Moody, that I love him.

Okay, maybe not that. Definitely not that.

But standing here backstage—my arm around the lovable yet slightly snot-nosed Rosa Johnson—while director-slash-theater-teacher Sonia Riverdale stares at me, her jaw dropped, is nearly as terrifying.

"Why, Shelby Phillips." The fifty-something with bleached blonde hair throws a well-manicured hand on a voluptuous hip. "You've been holding out on us."

I swallow, my gaze darting this way and that. We're now amassing a small crowd—mostly made of tiny people, sure, but still. They don't need to know that their stage manager can sing. It's irrelevant to them. And oh so embarrassing for me.

"Um." I cough. The overhead lights glare down on me, like a spotlight I don't want. Despite the air conditioning inside the K-8 school, my armpits begin to itch. "I don't know what you mean."

Little Rosa tugs on the bottom of my tank top. During the school year, I wouldn't dress so casually at work, but it's the summertime, and all forty or so people who are currently in the building are here working on Redmont Ridge's summer musical theater show, *Cinderella*.

Ignoring the weight of all the eyes on me, I squat to the six-year-old's level and squeeze her arm. "Yes, sweetie?"

"Thanks for singing with me." The smile she flashes holds no trace of the tremble from minutes ago, when I came upon her as she paced back and forth backstage, crying. "I think I know the right notes now."

A moment of peace wends through me. I suppose it was worth any embarrassment to help such sweetness shine. "Of course. Happy to help."

"You didn't just help." Sonia studies me as I stand again. "You inspired! You have a lovely voice. Why have I been relegating you to props and backstage management all these years when you've got those pipes on you?"

"That's where I like to be." And this is why I only ever sing in the closet, where I'm surrounded by jackets and sweaters to muffle the sound. Well, that and the shower. But that's not so weird. Everyone sings in the shower, right?

The point is, I do not perform in front of others—not since that memorable audition when I was twelve. But today, I broke my rule.

At least it was for an adorable reason.

Speaking of that reason, Rosa skips across the mostly empty stage to join a few friends who are occupying the auditorium's folding theater seats. Thankfully, the crowd has started to disperse, apparently bored by now. The ten or so adults who are either cast members or volunteer helpers are nowhere to be seen, while the kids —kindergartners all the way up to middle schoolers— continue taking advantage of our fifteen-minute rehearsal break. They practice dance steps, drink from colorful water bottles, play tag.

They're not affected in the least bit by what just happened. *Their* hearts probably aren't still sprinting at an unstoppable speed.

They aren't afraid to face the director.

But then there's me.

Sonia takes one more step in my direction, tapping her chin. "Don't think you're getting out of a lead role in next summer's show."

"Oh. Um." Is that all I know how to say? How about *"No way in the world will I ever get up on stage and sing again, thank you very much"*?

Unfortunately, I don't say things like that. Not out loud, anyway. Maybe I can simply fail to sign up to help with the show next year. I mean, sure, I've helped every one of the four summers since I've been a teacher here at the same San Diego school I attended myself. But I could take a—

Nope. Sigh. I know myself. I just can't do it. First of all, the summer arts program is always desperate for volunteers. Second, I love a good musical the way my housemate and friend Lauren loves 'N Sync. (Note: That's a lot. Like, she'd donate a kidney to Justin Timberlake if he asked for one.)

But perform? Sweat's breaking out on my forehead just at the thought of it.

Still, I have a whole year to practice saying no.

No. No. No. See? I can do it. I've got this.

Sonia gives me a nod—like it's a done deal—and walks away. So maybe I don't got this. My chest collapses as I inhale giant gobs of air.

Then someone slips an arm around my shoulders and said air is tinged with orange-vanilla cologne.

And once again, all is right with my world.

"Everything okay?" a low voice whispers in my ear.

I glance up at Eric, who is sporting his worn blue Padres hat backward. "Fine. Why?"

"No reason." He tugs the ends of my short blonde hair. "You just looked like a fish."

"A fish?"

Eric makes a face at me—bulging eyes, mouth in a round O. Then he sticks a hooked finger in the side of his mouth and tugs sideways.

Giggling, I shove him away. "That's so flattering. Thanks."

His blue eyes spark with mischief as he laughs and pokes me in the side.

I look around. "Where were you, anyway?"

"Painting sets just outside, of course. That's the job I was voluntold to do, remember?" He waggles his eyebrows at me.

My cheeks heat a bit. Yes, I may have begged him to help out this summer—and that would make me completely pathetic, except he's a middle school history teacher here as of last year, so it was totally legitimate for him to help out the arts program.

And spending time helping with a children's musical every day is exactly what every twenty-six-year-old man wants to do with his summer vacation, I'm sure. Ha. But Eric's a good guy.

The best guy.

Ugh. There I go again. I seriously *have* to find a way to get over him, or I'll be miserable for the rest of my life. And it's not as simple as writing him out of my life altogether. We've been best friends for seventeen years. My family is his family. My friends are his friends. And my life would be far *more* miserable without him in it.

"Yoohoo, Earth to Shelbs."

"Hmm?" Oh shoot, he's looking at me expectantly. I must have missed something. "How are the sets coming?"

"Fairly splendid, if I do say so myself."

"So modest." Though I'm honestly not surprised since Eric worked construction for seven years while putting himself through college. He's been teaching for a year.

"I only speak the truth." He bends his hand toward his chest, huffs on his fingernails, and scrubs them across his chest—which is currently covered in a tight blue paint-splattered T-shirt that's doing him all sorts of favors. His naturally athletic frame is exactly what I find attractive in a man. That, along with his brown hair that always has that adorably sexy "I just rolled out of bed" look, pretty much means he's the most handsome man I know. And his fun and sweet personality only makes him more good-looking.

But our years together have put me squarely in the friend zone—and even if Eric *did* want more, there are reasons we could never be. And while the thought of never being more than his best friend crushes my soul, all I need to truly be happy is for *him* to truly be happy.

And I know that, with me, he never really could be.

So I tolerate the zings of pleasure every time he touches me. The twisting of my heart whenever his smile is directed my way. The way warmth spills through my whole being when he sees me—really sees me—even when no one else does.

Like now. He's looking at me, a bit more seriously, head cocked to one side. "All right, what happened? Did Sonia say something rude? Because I will—" He makes a fist, hits it against the palm of his other hand, nods. "Well, not really, because I'm a gentleman and she's a woman. But I will have some seriously cutting words for her if she was mean to you."

"Stop." I tug his hands down, gripping them between my own. "I'm fine."

"Of course you are. You're the fabulous Shelby Phillips. The pied piper of small children. Men and women alike are putty in your hands!" His hands burst from my grip in a sweeping gesture. "Behold!" His voice raises and shouts as if thousands are listening to him.

Like always, he's got me grinning like a fool even as I'm rolling my eyes. "I've got to get back to work. And so do you. Those sets won't paint themselves." I start toward the props table, where I left my clipboard when I saw Rosa crying earlier. We pass a few kids leaning against a wall who are playing something on their tablets. They ignore us.

"Aw, come on, Shelbs." Eric keeps pace with me, pinching my elbow like a charmingly annoying dog nipping at my heels. "You know I hate painting with a passion. Give me a hammer and nails—good. A saw and sander. Even better. But the paint! Oh, the paint!"

"You're so dramatic. *You* should be the one Sonia's trying to get to perform."

"Wait, what?" He tugs on my arm, stopping me in my tracks and whirling me to face him. "That's what she wanted?"

"Yep." I wrinkle my nose. "Well, sort of." Snatching up the clipboard, I take a peek at my watch. Two more minutes till Sonia—who can be a fine arts drill sergeant when she wants to be—calls us to the stage again. Then I turn back to Eric, who is standing there with arms crossed over his chest, clearly still waiting for an answer. "She heard me singing, okay? I was helping Rosa with one of the songs."

A funny look comes across Eric's face. His jaw flexes a bit, his eyes widen ever so slightly, and he swallows. "You … sang? Like, in public?"

"Please don't make a big deal about this."

"But it is a big deal, right? You never sing. Ever. Like, every time your family does karaoke, and I beg you to duet with me, you wave your hand and tell me to sing my heart out. Which, of course, I do."

"You do." And it's always a sight to see him up there with my gaggle of nieces and nephews, wailing in the most awful falsetto along with Journey's "Don't Stop Believin'," jamming out like he has no qualms about failing in front of a crowd.

He and I couldn't be more opposite in that way, but it's one of the things I love about him. He just doesn't care what other people think—and I don't mean in an inconsiderate way. More in a "life's too short" way. And I get it. As a former foster kid who first lost his adoptive parents in a tragedy and then was carted from home to home after that, he's lived a lot of life. Much of it not good.

My life hasn't been a picnic either, but I don't have nearly the same seize-the-day courage that Eric does.

"I even use my adorable puppy dog eyes to try to get you to agree, but no dice." Eric leans in close, lowering his voice. "Now I know your secret."

I suppress a shiver. Because if he ever *did* know my real secret ... "And what's that?"

"You leave me no choice but to persuade one of your million nieces or nephews to help me convince you to sing at the next karaoke party. Children are your weakness. I don't know why I didn't think of it before."

"Won't work." I'm saying the words, but without

much conviction, because let's be honest—I'd be hard-pressed to say no to a kid. Especially one I'm related to.

Eric rubs his hands together, glee written all over his face. "Challenge accepted."

"You'd better n—"

At that moment, Sonia claps and we all scurry back to the auditorium, snagging seats so she can discuss what else we need to accomplish today. It's a lot, but with only a month left until the show opens (we've been at this about two weeks so far), there's still a fair amount to do.

When she calls the ensemble onto the stage, I decide to stay in my seat for a different view than I normally have on the sidelines. Sonia sometimes likes for me to watch from the audience and give her notes afterward, and it's not a problem because my assistant stage manager can handle things alone backstage for a bit.

Eric stays beside me too, his upper arm pressing against mine as we watch the cast practice one of the opening numbers they learned earlier this week. It's not terrible, but we've got a long way to go. I make some mental notes to help some of the younger ones cement the steps in their minds a bit better.

The scene shifts and now the prince is onstage talking with his parents. Sonia purposefully gave the roles with the most lines to adults, so hilariously, the prince is being played by a new teacher, Rob Stevens, while the king and queen are two seventh-graders half his size. I tap my foot along with the next song, lost in the story in the same way I've always been since my mom introduced me to movie musicals at the tender age of six—three years before she was diagnosed with a rare genetic disease that took her life two years later.

Of course, I grew up seeing her perform in live shows. She was dazzling, commanding the stage with her presence and her beautiful voice. I so wanted to be like that, but the one time I got brave enough to try …

I can feel Eric's eyes on me and turn. "What?" I whisper.

The corner of his lip turns upward. "It's just fun watching you." He says it in the same teasing way he always does whenever we watch *The Music Man* or *The Sound of Music* or any number of classic musical movies and I'm inevitably enraptured. "You're adorable."

Adorable. Just what every woman wants to be called by the man she's crazy about.

I tuck a piece of hair behind my ear and shrug. "I just love it."

He squeezes my knee twice before letting go. "I know."

I ignore the tremor pressing up my spine thanks to his lingering touch. We both turn our attention back to the stage, where the teacher playing Cinderella is doing her scene with the Fairy Godmother—nine-year-old Betsy McGrath. I had Betsy in my class as a kindergartner my first year teaching and she's just as boisterous and animated as I remember.

And that's why I really shouldn't be surprised when she accidentally flings her wand across the stage. But I gasp when it tumbles and twirls right into the eye of Cinderella—Janice Lovegood. Poor Janice staggers backward, clutching her eye ... and promptly falls off the stage into the orchestra pit below.

Eric jumps up from his spot beside me and races toward the stage while I just sit there, gripping the armrests, my heart screeching to a halt. Kids are screaming and rushing toward the edge of the pit to look over, while Sonia raises her hands and claps again in an attempt to commandeer their attention.

My gaze finally lands on Betsy, whose wide eyes are filling with tears. Oh no. I stand and hurry to the side ramp, taking it up to the stage and pulling her into my arms, shushing her and telling her it'll be okay.

"Sonia, you'd better call for an ambulance." Eric's voice drifts upward from the pit. "I think Janice might have broken her leg. We shouldn't move her."

Sonia whips out a phone. "Did she hit her head?"

"Thankfully, no. Doesn't seem like it."

"Hang on, Janice," Sonia calls, then pivots to hurry backstage. Probably so she can hear. The entire auditorium has broken out into pandemonium, and someone has to take charge.

I'm not normally that kind of person, but I wrangle six-year-olds for a living, so I can do it if need be.

Thankfully, I'm not the only adult here. There are a few parent and staff volunteers, plus Rob—aka The Prince—who jogs over to me. We've only spoken a handful of words to each other, but that doesn't matter now. He's also gone into teacher mode. "What's the plan? Should we have parents come early to pick everyone up?"

I bite my lip, considering. "Sonia might like to

resume practice after Janice is transported to the hospital. How about we take everyone out to the playground for a bit?"

He flashes me a thumbs-up. "Sounds good." Rob starts getting the few other adult volunteers' attention while I move to inform Sonia what's going on. She's still on the phone, however, so I take a moment to peek over the orchestra pit edge at Eric. He's sitting on the ground beside Janice, holding her hand and cracking jokes to get her to smile despite her obvious pain. He glances up at me, winks, then gives all his attention back to Janice.

I can't help the flutter in my chest.

"Shelby."

Pivoting, I find Sonia behind me, tapping her phone against her left palm. "Is the ambulance on the way?"

"Yes. I need to go meet them out front. And Janice's husband is going to meet *her* at the hospital." She stuffs her phone into the back pocket of her chinos and pinches the bridge of her nose. "I can only pray she doesn't sue the school."

Is that really what she's worried about? I place a hand on her upper arm. "I don't know Janice all that well, but she doesn't seem the type to sue. Everyone knows it was an accident." I take a beat before continuing. "Rob and I thought we'd take the kids to the playground, give the emergency crew room to work. Unless you want to just end practice?"

"I hate to lose a day of rehearsal, but I want to ride over with Janice. Leave no man—or woman, rather—behind, and all that."

"I completely understand. I'll have the children call

their parents to come to get them early, and I can stay with any kids whose parents we can't get ahold of."

"Perfect." Sonia tilts her head. "Walk with me, will you?"

"Just give me a minute." I jog back to Rob, let him know Sonia's decision, then tell him I'll be right back. After I rejoin Sonia, we start toward the side ramp and down into the auditorium, moving toward the back.

The director continues. "I'm no doctor, but I'm guessing this might put Janice out of commission for a while. She very likely won't be able to do the show."

"That's terrible. Hopefully it's not as bad as it seems. She makes such a good Cinderella." I push open the door from the auditorium into the theater building's foyer. The rays from the early July warmth—even in the summer, San Diego stays fairly temperate at only seventy-something degrees—travel through a bank of windows across from us as we amble through the empty space toward the doors that let out into the parking lot.

"She does. But do you know who *else* would make a good Cinderella?" The crash of the push bar echoes through the foyer as Sonia opens the door to the outside.

I purse my lips and step onto the walkway. A light salt-tinged breeze teases my hair, a reminder that we aren't that far from the ocean. "I'm not sure. The only other adults in the show are Juliet"—who is playing the Wicked Stepmother—"and ensemble members."

"The person I have in mind is not currently *in* the show." Sonia casts me a side glance.

In the distance, the whirr of an emergency vehicle grows louder.

"Oh!" I nod. "Samantha Quincy would be …" Oh wait. The fifth-grade teacher can't do it, can she? "But she's on a long vacation and won't be back in town until right before school begins again."

"This person is quite available." Sonia smiles at me, eyebrows raised.

An ambulance speeds into our parking lot. Its siren punctuates my thoughts, giving me a sudden headache. Sonia can't be saying what I think she's saying. "You don't mean—"

"I do." She takes my hands in hers. "You would be the ideal Cinderella. You're petite, sweet as apple pie, blonde—and girl, can you sing! Plus I know you've already learned the music and the dance steps so far just by watching us."

"B-but seeing them and doing them are two different things. And I don't know all the lines." Not to mention the fact that I DON'T SING IN PUBLIC.

"So you'll learn them. You have a month."

"But—"

"Hold that thought."

A man and woman jump from the ambulance and Sonia waves them over. "This way." She leaves me standing there on the sidewalk, and I'm pretty sure an angler fish has nothing on my dropped-jaw expression.

I don't move—can't move—until the paramedics carry Janice out on a stretcher. Eric and Sonia come out behind them, and once they have Janice settled in the back, Eric shoots me a wave and jumps in with Janice. He'll be good medicine for her.

Sonia, whose purse is slung over her shoulder, faces

me again. "I've got to go, but think about what I've said, all right? I'll text you with Janice's condition once we know more and we can go from there. Good? Good." Without waiting for a reply, she waltzes toward her Red Mustang.

"No, Sonia," I whisper to her shadow. "Not good. Not good at all."

two

. . .

"I CAN'T BELIEVE you told her yes." Eric leans around me to snatch a cherry tomato off the veggie platter I'm arranging in my dad and stepmom's kitchen.

When he reaches for another, I smack his hand playfully and finish transferring the last few from the strainer to the plate that's the shape of a carrot. "What else could I say?"

"Oh, I don't know, Shelbs. There's this other word in the English language. Starts with an N, ends with an O. Let's say it together. Nooooooo."

I pick up the tray and walk it to the large granite-topped island. "The show literally can't go on without a Cinderella." It's been two days since the accident. Yesterday, Sonia called me with the news that Janice's leg is in traction and she needs me to step up.

"But why does it have to be you?"

"Why does what have to be Shelby?" My stepmom

Frannie chooses that moment to enter the kitchen carrying a platter of burgers my dad grilled up out back. We normally have a fancier meal for our Sunday family lunches—pot roast or lasagna, Frannie's specialty—but since tomorrow is the Fourth of July, Dad wanted to do a cookout.

"Shelby is—"

"Nothing." I shoot him my version of a glare, which Eric has jokingly called as scary as a puppy dog baring its tiny teeth.

Frannie pushes her silver bangs out of her eyes and lifts a thin eyebrow. Despite her sixty-three years, her face is nearly wrinkle free, and she works out more than I do (which is just about never, unless you count chasing six-year-olds around). Her gold Seiko watch glints from her wrist. "Doesn't sound like nothing."

"What doesn't?" In comes my dad, joined at the hip with my oldest brother, Joseph, who is forty to my twenty-six. "Hi, sweetie." Dad removes his grilling gloves and leans over to kiss me on the cheek. His more salt than pepper mustache tickles my skin.

Before I can give an answer, a tornado of screams and laughter bursts through the back door and a majority of my thirteen nephews and nieces race inside. The youngest—babies Penny and Nick and two-year-old Timmy—are brought in by their mothers (two of my four sisters-in-law), who are chatting about the trials of breastfeeding.

The noise level has risen to an extreme degree, and this isn't even all of my twenty-five family members, as my older sister Deb hasn't yet arrived. But there's the doorbell and Dad's German Shepherd Laney starts barking like an attack is imminent and I just lean my hip against the counter and catch Eric smirking at me, shaking his head.

Though he lives alone and is used to a nice quiet existence, he loves these chaotic family gatherings as much as I do. We met on the playground when we were nine years old. Mom had just been diagnosed with her condition, and Eric had just been moved to a new foster family after losing his adoptive parents in a car accident at seven. (All he knows about his bio parents is that his dad left before he was born and his mom died of a drug overdose when he was a baby. He has good memories, though few, of his parents who adopted him when he was one.)

In each other, we found the friend the other needed, and he started coming over to my house for nearly every family function. I think my parents would have considered adopting him if Mom hadn't gotten sick—a strange thought considering how I feel about him now. Of course, those feelings didn't really develop until high school, so if he'd become my brother before then, they never would have manifested in the first place.

Still. Weird.

Deb, her husband James, and her kids—sassy pants Delilah, studious Barrett, and rough and tumble little Elise—tromp through the front door and give a round of hugs and hellos. The kiddos run off to join their cousins, who have moved into the living room where the Nintendo Switch is set up.

At twelve years my senior, Deb looks more and more

like our mom every day. She's got the same brown curls, the same long neck, same fiery hazel eyes. Other than my five-foot-four-inch stature, I look much more like my dad's side of the family with my short blonde bob, pale skin, small nose, and blue eyes.

My sister comes around the counter and grabs me into a hug. "What did I miss?" Her family was out of town visiting James's family last Sunday, so they missed our weekly gathering.

"Shelby was just about to tell us some news." Frannie's eyes shine with something akin to amusement. She and my dad have been married for eleven years, when I was just fifteen and the only of my siblings still at home since Cody had just left for college. It was hard at first, seeing him with someone other than my mom. But he explained to me that he and Mom had such a wonderful marriage, and while no one could ever replace her in his heart, he was ready to find another companion who could be a partner. And I mean, he was only fifty years old. Who was I to tell him he had to be alone for the rest of his life?

But however much I like Frannie—love her, really—I do not appreciate her in this moment. "No I wasn't."

"Ooo, let me guess." Levi's wife Lisa grabs a Dorito from one of the chip bowls on the island. "You and Eric are finally together."

The whole family cracks up, the joke that's been bandied about for years apparently still not as old as it should be.

My eyes flash to Eric, but instead of appearing

uncomfortable, he just grins. "I've told you guys. She just won't give in to me, no matter how much I beg."

However much I wish the words were true, I know he's just playacting so my family doesn't bug us further on the subject. I'm honestly grateful he's taking the attention off of me.

But it doesn't last long because Frannie clucks her tongue. "Well, there's definitely something secret going on." She fluffs the salad with a pair of tongs.

Ugh. Fine. "I'm going to play Cinderella in our school musical at the beginning of August."

The laughter dies and my siblings all gape at me. A chunk of hard-boiled egg falls off the chip Joseph has dipped into the potato salad. The only sound is the muffled noise of Mario Kart racing in the room next door.

"You're in a play?" My sister-in-law Jenny's voice cracks the silence.

"Not just that … you're the lead?" Deb bites her lip and her eyes suddenly look a bit misty.

Oh my goodness, toss some water on my cheeks, because they're burn burn burning right about now. "Um, yep." I straighten the slivers of bell pepper lining the veggie tray, even though they're really not all that crooked.

"That's great, honey." Dad slips his arm around my shoulders and squeezes. "Mom would be proud."

A tear falls down my cheek before I can stop it. I grasp the silver locket I'm always wearing—once upon a time, it was Mom's—and rub my thumb along the smooth surface. "Thanks, Dad."

It takes a few seconds, but my siblings all rush to agree with Dad. Then Frannie announces it's time for lunch and someone gets the kids. Dad says a quick prayer of thanks and it's a scramble of people all getting plates of food and taking them out to the back deck, where Dad and Frannie have a glorious view of the San Diego hills and three long picnic tables.

I stand back, arms crossed, my insides still quivering. Meanwhile, Eric and my brother Byron taunt each other about this afternoon's football game, declaring to the other who is going to win. My oldest nephews Dylan and Jeremy join in, fake punching Eric while a few of my nieces tug on his arms asking for a piggyback ride. Sometimes I think my family loves Eric more than they do me. That doesn't make me feel sorry for myself, though. It just makes me so glad he has a place in this world—and it is blessedly with the other people I love most.

"Hey." Deb sidles up to me. "So what made you decide to do this show? You've never shown interest in performing before."

She doesn't know about the flopped audition years ago. "It's less of a decision and more of a necessity." I explain about Janice's accident.

"Well, I'm proud of you. I know it's been hard for you to sing since Mom died."

"You know I used to sing?" And love it even still …

"Of course. Don't you remember those family gatherings before she got sick? Mom would coax you out of your shell, get you to sing a bit with her. But you'd only sing with her. No one else."

"That's right." I barely squeak out the words. I'd almost forgotten those times. I was young, after all.

The kitchen clears out and Deb and I grab plates. Frannie always makes a ton of food and everyone chips in, bringing a side dish, but I have to laugh at how depleted things are—and how messy the scene is now. Dribbles of baked bean juice, crushed chips, and smushed mustard adorn the countertop. It reminds me of that scene in *Seven Brides for Seven Brothers* when Millie flips the table because the brothers are eating like hogs.

"So." Deb snags a hamburger bun, opens it, and places it on her plate. "I noticed you didn't laugh at Lisa's comment. In fact, you never do whenever someone teases about you and Eric."

My spine stiffens but I shovel a spoonful of macaroni salad onto my plate and keep moving through the food line regardless. "I never know what to say."

"Because you love him, right?"

I freeze. "Of course I love him." Sandpaper grit coats my throat. "He's my best friend."

Deb lifts her eyebrow and gives me her mom look. "That's not what I mean and you know it." She turns her attention toward doctoring up her burger with relish, ketchup, lettuce, and tomato. "I can see right through you."

As much as I suspect some of my family members— my friends too—know how I feel about Eric, no one has ever come right out and accused me of loving him like … that. But I shouldn't be surprised my sister would be the one to finally do it. She's a shrink, after all.

Plus, even after thirteen years of marriage, she's still desperately in love with her husband and believes everyone should find a match as great as hers.

Deb continues as if she hasn't just rocked my equilibrium. "You've been waiting around for him while he dated bimbo after bimbo in high school. At least his choices in college were much more acceptable, even if they never lasted long. Meanwhile you …"

"Hardly dated at all?"

"Exactly. I know you're shy, but I think it's been more than that. You're hung up on Eric."

Dang, my sister is perceptive. Her clients must love her.

"Deb—"

"He's been without someone for like a year now." When she's on a roll, she can't be stopped, so I just keep quiet while she finishes her thoughts. "So here's your chance, Shelby. What if he meets someone else while you're busy deciding to be brave?"

Brave … that's all I want to be. Brave like Mom. But in this case, bravery has meant something else entirely.

My hand shakes as I set down the spoon. "Even if I did"—I dart a glance toward the back door, making sure the coast is clear—"love him, it wouldn't matter. He wants a family."

"And you don't? You'll be an amazing mom someday, Shelby. Look at how great you are with your students, with all of our crazy kids."

"I know. I mean, I do want a family. But …" I inhale. "I can't have one. Naturally, I mean."

"What?" Deb's nose crinkles. "How do you know if you've never tried?"

I can see that I'm only confusing her. Biting the inside of my cheek, I speak the words I've never told anyone. "I don't mean that I can't. Only that I won't." A pause. "I got tested, Deb."

"Oh." Her gaze falls, right into the potato salad in front of her. Then she looks up at me again. "You have the gene?"

With a small nod, I confirm the beast that's been sitting on my chest for the last eight years—ever since my eighteenth birthday, when I could finally get the test to confirm whether I carried the same mutated gene my mom had.

Mom might not have known she had the gene until after she had kids—after all, her disease onset didn't happen until she was in her forties, a rarity considering the disease normally hits babies and toddlers—but I *do* know. And I refuse to potentially subject anyone to the horrors the neurological disorder entails. At the end, Mom was bound to a wheelchair, unable to feed herself. She went deaf in one ear, blind in one eye. It was one thing after another, and I was only nine, so I'm sure I didn't even fully understand the whole picture back then.

"I'm a carrier," I say. "I won't end up with the disease myself, but I could pass it on to my kids."

"I'm sorry, sis." Deb wraps me in a hug, and her lavender scent surrounds me. I know if anyone understands what I'm feeling, it's her—although her own test came back negative. It's why she felt comfortable having children. "But there's more than one way to have a family, Shelby. If Eric is the one for you, he would understand."

I bury my face in her shoulder and my whole body shudders with the need to release all the emotions I've kept pent up for so long. "I know for a fact he wants biological kids, Deb. He told me once."

Sure, we were sixteen when we wished on a star and told each other our deepest desires, but Eric wouldn't change his mind about that. It was too important to him —to finally have someone in his life who shares his DNA. His blood. He's gone most of his life without it, and even his place in my family won't give him that.

My sister pulls back, cocks her head. "Shelby—"

The back door slides open behind us. "Hey. Oh, sorry."

I turn to find Eric there. His eyes ask me what's wrong. I blink, give my head a little shake to tell him I'm fine. But *he* doesn't look fine, if the way he's fiddling with his ball cap brim is any indication.

"Think about what I said, okay?" Deb grabs her plate. "I'd better make sure James doesn't need any assistance with the wild animals out back."

After she leaves, I step forward and place a hand on Eric's upper arm. "What's wrong?"

"First, are you okay? Looked like I was interrupting something."

I shake my head. "I'm fine. You?"

He lets out a breath. "Just got a call from my super. My apartment flooded. Something about pipes bursting in the apartment above me."

"Oh no. How bad is it?"

"Uninhabitable." Eric tilts his head to the sky, groans. "He said it looked like the things in my upper closet are okay, but otherwise it might be a total loss."

Poor guy. But at least the family photo albums he has are probably safe. The other stuff is just stuff—he learned early on not to get attached to things.

But another thought strikes me. "So do they have another apartment for you?"

Eric shrugs. "I don't know. I've got to go. Sorry to miss Sunday lunch."

"You'll make the next one. Of course you need to get over there." I scurry to the front entryway with him and snag the keys out of my purse, unloosing the key to the house I share with Alexis and Lauren. My former housemates, Evie and Kayla, both got married late last year and now live with their husbands, Connor and Josh. "Here." I press it into his palm.

"What's this?"

"My house key. You're staying with us."

His lips curl in amusement. "Not sure Alexis will like me sleeping on her precious couch."

"Well, good thing Lauren happens to be out of the country visiting Topher in Kentonia." Lauren's boyfriend is a straight up actual prince, and she's spending almost all of July with him and his family at their palace. "I'm sure she wouldn't mind you crashing in her room."

"And you don't think Alexis would mind?"

"No." While my housemate—and owner of the house—is prickly on the outside, she really does care about her friends. And though she pretends to be staunch in her belief that "all men are pigs," I think she considers Eric, Topher, Connor, and Josh exceptions to that rule. "Besides, I pay rent, so I have some say in the matter."

Eric lifts an eyebrow. "Look at you, standing up for yourself. Good for you, Shelbs."

"Stop. You know I'd do anything for you. And this isn't that much. Just a place to stay."

He sighs. "I'd argue with you, but I really need to go. Who knows what they're doing with my stuff right now." Eric holds up the key. "But thank you. I'll take you up on the offer and be out of your hair in no time."

"You won't be in my hair." We spend a ton of time together as it is.

"You don't know that." He pokes me and leans in for a quick hug. "You've never lived with me before."

The thought does something funny to my stomach, making it jump and turn like the notes of a lilting melody I can't quite grasp. "It'll be fun. More time to watch musicals," I tease him. The poor man has watched his fair share over the course of our friendship.

"Suddenly, sleeping in a flooded apartment doesn't sound so bad."

"Ha ha. Get out of here." I turn him around and give him a push toward the door.

He laughs all the way out, and as I watch him walk to his Jeep, I can't help but wonder if he's right. Not that he will be in my hair, but what if living together—even for a few weeks—changes things between us? Or, worse, what if it makes it even more difficult to deny the pull I have toward him?

I slam the door shut. I'll just have to be stronger than the pull.

Because what Eric wants matters more than anything I might feel. And what he wants, I can't give him.

three

. . .

"COME ON, ALEXIS." I poke my head into the master suite of our three-bedroom Point Loma bungalow. "Time to go."

Alexis Matkin, who is sitting at her bright pink desk with her back to me, holds up a finger as she hovers over her laptop. "Sec. I have to finish my thought on this design."

Her long hair is in three braids—one died red, one white, and one blue in honor of Independence Day today. Yesterday, it was purple. You just never know with her.

I move inside her bedroom. "Is this the McMahon project?"

Her eyes narrow in on her laptop, where there's a colorful logo design that's different than the one I saw yesterday. "Mmm."

Okaaaay. I glance at the clock, which resembles one

of those clear phones from the nineties—the see-through ones with the colorful wires inside. Much like her hair, the rest of Alexis's room is a variety of colors, and between the lime green comforter, the hot pink furniture, and the yellow abstract artwork on the walls, it looks like an artist's palette threw up in here. Then again, she's a graphic artist so I suppose I shouldn't be surprised that her space is the opposite of my pastel purple room.

I touch her shoulder. "We've got to go now or Kayla will murder us with her eyes when we show up."

She snorts. "Ain't that the truth." Finally, she clicks save and shuts the laptop lid, rubbing her eyes. "Sorry. I was up till three last night fixing the design, but ended up sick of it, so started something fresh this morning. It just has to be the best, you know?"

"I know." Not only does she take her work very seriously, but she's competing for a big client with a guy from her office—a guy she vehemently hates. Sometimes I wonder if she protests about Dax a little too much, but I don't dare risk saying so. "Come on. You're not even dressed."

She glances down at her jeans and Beatles T-shirt. "What's wrong with what I'm wearing?"

I run a hand down my new pink swimsuit cover up, which hits mid-thigh—far shorter than I'd normally feel comfortable wearing, but I just loved the cute lacy coverlet so much that I didn't care. "We're headed to the beach, remember? Connor's bringing food? We're watching fireworks? Playing volleyball?"

"I'd rather stay here and work. All of those people." She shudders. "You know I hate crowds."

I laugh and pull on her arm until she stands. Then I point toward her dresser and use my kindergarten teacher voice—gentle but firm. "Come on. Grab your bathing suit, get dressed, and Eric and I will meet you at the front door."

"Fiiiiine."

For all her grouching, Alexis thankfully wasn't against Eric staying with us for a while. She may have lifted a purple eyebrow and asked if I was sure that was a good idea—to which I pretended I had no idea what she meant and replied "of course"—but she is a good friend. Loyal. Stubborn, but loyal.

I close her door behind me and walk down the hallway toward the living room, where I find Eric scrolling his phone on the blue couch in his red bathing suit, white T-shirt, Padres hat, and flip-flops. Thankfully his clothes were hanging in his closet and thus weren't affected by the flooding in his apartment, so he brought an entire suitcase with him last night.

He glances up and fumbles the phone. Eric's nostrils flare as he reaches toward the floor for it. "New outfit?" His voice pitches just slightly. Someone else might not pick up on it, but this is Eric we're talking about.

"Yeah." I smooth the edge of the skirt, the material rough under my fingertips. "I found it on sale."

"It's … nice." He coughs.

"Thanks."

Times like this—when I swear he maybe finds me

attractive—I wonder if he feels the same way about me as I do about him. Of course, it's not like he's ever said so or made a move. It's really easy to get in my head about it, going round and round.

But then I remember that it doesn't matter. Answering that question will only do more harm than good.

So I pretend I don't notice, and I do my best not to store away the memories, the little moments of imagined attraction between us. I pinch my fingers into my palm and remind myself that he's my best friend and that's as good as it will ever be between us and that I'm lucky to have such an amazing best friend in the first place. Some people don't even have that much.

I take a breath. "Alexis is almost ready to go."

"Cool." He stands and slides his phone into his pocket. "I'm gonna grab a water. You want one?"

"Sure, thanks."

A few seconds later, Alexis appears in terry shorts, a tank top, and sandals. "All right, let's get this shindig on the road."

Eric rejoins us and hands me a water. Then we all head outside, pile into Eric's Jeep, and chat while he drives to Ocean Beach. After circling the lot for a decent while, we luck out when a truck leaves a space and Eric sneaks in. We grab our beach bags, chairs, and Eric's boogie board and walk toward the spot we prearranged to meet up with our friends, who are already here. The beach is hopping with people of all colors, shapes, sizes, and ages.

When we step onto the sand, I pull off my flip-flops

and thread them between my fingers. We pass a few kids eating ice cream on sticks, the blue-colored treat dripping in rivulets down their chins. Some college-aged students toss a Frisbee nearby, an older gentleman with a wide-brimmed hat sets up a bright green umbrella, and a few women in bikinis sunbathe face-down on their towels. A man passes by on the board-walk, a speaker blaring rap music that's there and gone in a few seconds. It's early afternoon, the sun is shining without a trace of clouds in the sky, and the ocean crashes in greeting. Not much can get me down today.

Well, except for my looming first day of rehearsal as Cinderella tomorrow.

"Don't ruin the memory of today with worries about tomorrow." My mom's voice echoes in my mind, one of the few clear, crisp memories I have of just her and me, together.

I spot the Bryants and Gregorys a little ways down the beach and point them out to Eric and Alexis. We weave our way through the sand until we're with our friends, who have set up three umbrellas and spread out a couple of huge beach blankets.

A shirtless Connor is sitting up on his knees, digging through a large picnic basket and pulling out containers that are sure to contain delicious food he made. Evie is sitting in a chair beside him in a one-piece bathing suit and black cover up. Her brown hair is piled on top of her head and she's fanning herself with a paper plate. I wonder if she's coming down with something, because it's not that hot out here and yet she has a line of sweat beading along her forehead.

Kayla is leaning back against her husband, Josh, who says something in her ear that has her laughing and wiping her eyes. It won't be the same without Topher and Lauren here today, but we've set up a time to call them later.

Evie is the first to spot us. "Hey, guys!" She starts to stand, but her cheeks pale slightly and she sits back down quickly. Huh.

I get there first and bend down to give her and Kayla hugs. Eric fist bumps Josh and Connor, while Alexis plops into the sand and grunts hello to everyone. When Connor tells us to snag a plate and eat, he doesn't have to tell Eric twice. The guy can seriously put it away. All the guys can.

We chat about the latest as we eat. Connor's first novel is hitting shelves next month. Evie's job at the publishing company is keeping her extra busy because her boss is on a month-long vacation. And Kayla's dating coach business is thriving, so much so that she's quitting her job at Java Awakening, where Josh is the manager.

"He's really going to miss our private business meetings in his office," Kayla says with a twinkle in her eye.

"Leia." Josh coughs and turns as red as a sunburn while Connor and Eric heckle him and Alexis rolls her eyes. I, on the other hand, think it's adorable how much they love each other, how Kayla embarrasses Josh with her public displays of affection.

Evie pushes her food around on her plate—has she even take a bite?—and smiles. "Let's keep it PG, huh, Kay? There are little ears nearby."

"What? We *do* talk business stuff!" Kayla nudges her husband in the ribs. "Sometimes."

Then, out of the blue, her eyes turn watery and she sniffles. "I actually really *am* going to miss it. Being with you every day. Seeing you make a sexy latte day in and day out."

Josh's eyes widen behind his glasses and then his top lip curls.

"Am I the only one who doesn't know what a sexy latte is?" I whisper to Eric before taking a bite of fried chicken, which is crunchy and delicious.

"Don't ask." Alexis pretends to plug her ears. "We do not need to know this information. And Kayla, why are you crying about that? Pretty sure you wouldn't cry at a funeral."

"Harsh!" Connor says before taking a giant bite of fruit salad.

"You don't think I'd cry at a funeral?" That sets Kayla off again, and all of us are looking at each other, bewildered. Because while Alexis is definitely overstating Kayla's lack of crying prowess, she is right that the times Kayla has showcased her true emotions are few and far between.

There's a bit of an awkward lull in the conversation, and I pretty much hate that more than almost anything. So I do what needs to be done—I fill it. "Did I tell you guys that I'm playing the lead role in the children's musical at school next month? Nope? Well, I am."

"What?!" Kayla swipes furiously at her tears. "How did that happen?"

Once again, I tell the tale, pushing a spare tomato

around on the top of my salad. In the distance, a seagull swoops and snatches a sandwich off the unwatched plate of a toddler, who sees the loss and begins to wail. *I understand, kid. I really do.*

"Wow. That's incredible. I knew you liked musicals, but not that you liked to sing." Evie sets her full plate aside and places her hand against her stomach.

"What Evie is saying politely is we had no idea you *could* sing." Alexis leans back on her hands and the tips of her braids brush the sand.

"I don't really know that I can."

"I'm sure you can. Your director wouldn't have cast you if you couldn't. You're going to do great, Shelbs." Kayla leans forward and squeezes my hand. "I just … know it." Then she is full-on sobbing and Josh pulls her back into his arms.

Alexis narrows her eyes and gestures toward Kayla. "Okay, what's the freaking deal here? Why is Kayla losing her stuff? Did she start drinking early today?"

"I'm … not … drinking … at … all." Kayla hiccups. "That's … the … problem."

Wait. It's a holiday and Kayla isn't drinking? Not that she's a lush by any means, but she's always the first one to crack open a wine cooler at a party. "Kayla …" I bite the inside of my cheek. "Are you …?"

She nods. "Yeah."

Josh smiles.

"Oh my goodness!" I launch myself at my friend and hug her first, then Josh. "I'm so happy for you guys."

"Am I the only one who's confused?" Eric's voice drifts from behind me.

"She's pregnant, duh." And that would be Alexis, who nudges me aside so she can also give Kayla a hug. She pulls back, looks strangely at Kayla's stomach, and shakes her head. "This is so weird."

"Wanna know what's even weirder?" Connor pipes up. It takes me a second to turn and realize that he and Evie haven't moved from their spots on the other side of the circle—which is ultra strange, because Evie and Kayla are best friends. If anyone should be shouting for joy, it's Evie.

And there is definitely a serene smile on Evie's face, and yes, tears too—though that's fairly usual for her.

Connor grabs Evie's hand and looks at her like he's Harold Hill and she's Marian Paroo. A love match if I ever did see one.

Evie's pale cheeks color a bit as she surveys all of us. "I'm pregnant too."

"No way!" That sets Kayla off again, but she walks on her knees the short distance to Evie and tackles her in a hug. "Our babies are gonna be besties. They have to be. Just like their"—*sob*—"mamas." They're a puddle of crying messes on the sand and I wonder how we must look to any observers.

The rest of the afternoon passes in a flash, with Kay and Evs talking about their terrible morning sickness, weird hormonal urges, and due dates (Evie around New Year's and Kayla just a week later). You wouldn't know they're both growing life inside of them, especially Kayla, whose bikini-clad body doesn't show even a hint of a bump.

And there's a moment—okay, more than one—

where I have to grab fistfuls of sand at my side to keep something ugly from flaring inside of me. In my family, I've been around plenty of pregnant women, but this is the first time one of my best friends is pregnant … and it's two of them at once! I wouldn't be surprised if Lauren comes home from Kentonia engaged, and then it'll be wedding bells and baby cradles for her and Topher too.

Yes, all of my friends are in their early thirties, several years older than me, but life marches on. And for the first time, I take a real look at my situation. I've known for the last eight years that I would never have a biological child—that I couldn't even entertain the thought—and it's caused me heartache because it meant I couldn't be with Eric.

But I think … I'm realizing now … that I forgot to mourn the actual loss of a dream. Because I've always wondered what it would feel like, to have life flutter inside of me. To experience the miracle of childbirth. To ask my husband in the middle of the night to get me Skittles. (Not that I'd ever actually do that. Probably. But who knows? Maybe pregnancy hormones would make me a totally different person. Case in point: Kayla.)

Before I have time to contemplate much more, Eric tugs me up and into a game of beach volleyball. I have to grind my teeth when he whips off his shirt—a glorious sight I've seen more times than I can count over the years and yet never tire of—and try to give all my focus to the game, which I'm terrible at. (Other than ice skating and dancing, I'm basically allergic to anything athletic.)

It's a whirlwind of a day, and when it's finally dark and time for fireworks, we all sit together on blankets near the pier. The sun has disappeared and with it, the warmth of the day. I'm wearing Eric's sweatshirt, as I forgot my own, and the feel of its worn cotton is as familiar as that of my own sweatshirt (because I've commandeered it, again, more times than I can count).

It's been a lovely day, but the news of my friends' double pregnancies, along with what tomorrow will bring, now weighs me down as I finally sit. The first firework shoots into the air and the crowd oohs and aahs. Someone nearby plays patriotic music from a phone and my ears catch strands of "God Bless America."

Eric and I sit arm to arm as we watch pinks, greens, blues, oranges, and every color of the rainbow explode in the sky, a reminder of triumph. Of beauty. Of freedom.

And it's a weak moment, but I allow myself this one and lay my head on his shoulder.

He's quiet for a good while, though I feel his steady breaths lift and lower his chest, his shoulder, my head. Then, finally, "You're sad."

It takes me a long moment to answer. "Not exactly."

"What then?"

He doesn't know about my genetics. Doesn't know about my struggle, my decision. We talk about almost everything, but not that. Never anything that has to do with us. The possibility of what could be. And for me, the genetics tie in with *him* more than I can even understand.

So I go with the far easier answer. "The show. I … I don't know if I can do it, Eric."

"Well, I do." He places a hand on my knee, his thumb drawing circles there. Oh, how I wish I could take that hand, *really* take it in mine. Embrace all that he might be offering me. Not that he's ever actually done so.

Another firework rocks the sky, splitting it open before a volley of rockets goes off—blindingly white, pure, lovely.

"How can I help?"

"I'm not sure if you can." Though he's so sweet to offer.

"There has to be something." He turns his head, kisses my temple, and I can feel his warm breath all the way to my toes. "How about running lines with you? Would that help?"

It might, actually. And yet … "You have better things to do with your time than that."

"Shelbs."

There's a moment of rawness, realness, in his tone. It draws me upright, where I can look into his eyes. And even though it's dark, I see something there. Something I'm not prepared for. That I have to be imagining.

Devotion. True and long and deep. Possibly more than the kind a man would have for his best friend.

"What?" I can't help the tremble in my voice, because I'm asking, but I don't want to know.

I don't think I do, anyway.

"Don't you know I'd do anything for you?"

The fireworks finale rages on and my heart aches.

Because I do know. I'd do the same for him—even push him away when I just want to hold him close. I lean back, smile, and force ugly words out of my mouth. "Thanks, Eric. You're such a good friend."

Emphasis on the word *friend*.

Because that's all we can ever be.

four

· · ·

NORMALLY, I love the energy of rehearsals.

Sonia alternately sitting in the front row giving critiques and bouncing around the stage blocking scenes and showing the actors where to stand, how to move, where to look.

Children chattering when they aren't supposed to and nearly missing their entrances. Flashing me the biggest gap-toothed smiles ever when they ask to borrow a prop they know they aren't going to get.

The distant sound of drills and hammers as the stage-building crew works on the other side of the garage-like door that rolls open between the backstage and the concrete outdoor slab.

Lilting music that threads its way through the entire auditorium until it hits the stage and the actors become part of the song.

But today, I'm supposed to be part of the energy—a main part, not an observant side piece like I'm used to.

And that's something I just don't know how to do.

"All right." Sonia huffs out a sigh from her spot in the front row. Her lips purse as she taps her clipboard with a pencil. "Let's take it from the top. Again."

I wince at her last word, a clear dig at me. Or maybe I'm just being extra sensitive. I wouldn't blame her if she was frustrated with me. My eyes are super dry—I forgot to take out my contacts last night—and my hands are shaking so badly that I keep losing my place in the script. Not only that, but every time I speak, my voice sounds like one of Cinderella's mice. Sonia keeps yelling at me to "Project!"

Rob, who is standing opposite me at center stage, holds himself with an easy confidence that reminds me of Eric. He's probably in his early thirties, with short blond hair that's gelled to perfection. And though his brown eyes are not arresting like Eric's blue ones, they *are* kind.

Which is something I really need right now as my insides twist and I'm fairly certain I might lose what little breakfast I managed to choke down.

"Hey." He leans closer, cups my elbow. His eyebrows form a V. "You're doing great."

"Thank you. I just feel like I'm majorly screwing this up." I take a peek around us. We are currently surrounded by the ensemble cast, as everyone has taken their places for the scene where Cinderella and the Prince meet for the first time at the ball.

All eyes are on me for the second rehearsal in a row. They're mostly kids and kids see things through different lenses than adults. They don't expect perfection. They just want to know that you see them. And I want to show them that we can all do hard things. Want to be an example. But right now, I don't feel like anyone's example. I just feel like that scared twelve-year-old girl who lost first her mom and then her voice.

And I haven't even had to attempt singing yet.

Black dots swim in front of my face. The fluorescents seem to flicker overhead. Oh, goodness. I might faint.

Rob must sense this, because he slides his arm around my waist to support me. "Breathe, Shelby. Stop locking your knees. It's going to be fine."

I allow myself to lean into him and relax my posture, especially my knees. How did he realize I was standing at stiff attention when I didn't even know it?

"There you go. Good job." Rob squeezes my waist.

My ears are buzzing and I think I hear Sonia telling everyone to take fifteen, children scattering. I release another breath and straighten a bit, though I do not go back to my soldier pose. "Thanks."

"No problem." Rob doesn't release me, though he does loosen his hold a tad. "I'm the choir teacher, remember? I've seen my fair share of faintings."

I chuckle. "Makes sense."

"I've also seen my fair share of stage fright."

My gaze sharply meets his. He's not overly tall by most standards—but nearly everyone is taller than me—and so doesn't have to look way down his nose at me. His smile is open, friendly.

"How could you tell?" I whisper. "Do you think everyone else knows?"

"Nah. I've just been in the performing arts my whole life. I get nervous too."

"Really?" Nothing about him seems that way, but appearances can totally be deceiving, I suppose. "How do you get past it?"

"I'm not sure you do. You just lean into it instead. Remember that you love this—if not everything that comes with it, surely there's something you love."

I nod. "Music. The way it moves both airwaves and people."

Something crosses his features, flashing in his eyes. Something like admiration. Attraction? No. A charismatic guy like him would never be attracted to a mousy teacher like me.

But before I can analyze it, the flash of emotion on his face is replaced with his genial smile once more. "I couldn't agree more, and I look forward to dueting with you."

"Oh. Right." I stare at the ground. "The thing is, I don't sing in public. Ever."

His hand finally drops from my waist and he pushes that same hand through his hair. "I'm sure you're great." Then he winks at me—and while it surprises me, it does nothing for me. Not like Eric's wink from the orchestra pit on Friday. "But I'm happy to give you some private singing lessons if you want some help." He quickly groans. "Wow, that sounded kind of creepy, didn't it?"

I chuckle. "Maybe it would if I didn't know you were a nice guy."

"I'm glad you think so." His cheeks tinge a bit red. "I

promise I was just offering to help. If, you know, it would be helpful."

Aw, he's sweet. "It might be great, actually." If I'm going to be forced to sing in public, at least some lessons would help me with my technique. Make it more bearable. "Thanks."

"No problem. Anything for my lovely co-star." He leans in, squeezes my elbow again. "I'll be right back. Need to check on something in my office while we've got a break."

"Of course." Still smiling, I turn, determined to find a quiet corner to run through my lines for this scene with no one watching me. Ironically, I find something else instead—or, should I say, someone.

Eric stands just off stage, hands shoved into his pockets, eyes narrowed as they follow Rob across the stage and through the back door that connects the backstage with the hallway into the fine arts building. I haven't seen him scowl like that since the Padres didn't make the playoffs. Before I can head over and ask him what's going on, he leaves, presumably heading back to the set building area.

What was *that* all about?

Later in the afternoon, when we duck into his Jeep on the way home, I'm too tired and wrung out to ask him how he's doing. It's seriously all I can do to not break down into tears over that rehearsal. Because while I did survive it, it continued to be brutal. Now a headache pounds behind my eyes and all I want to do is drown my sorrows in *Singin' in the Rain*, a musical that never fails to make me smile with its romance and charm.

So I do.

A few hours later, there's a knock on my bedroom door. With my laptop in front of me, I'm lying stomach first on the queen bed I inherited from Deb when she and James upgraded to a king a few months ago. My legs are kicked in the air behind me and I'm starting to regret my "dinner" of an entire bag of Skittles (and not the small bag—the size meant for sharing) and a tall glass of white wine.

The knock sounds again. "Shelbs."

It's Eric.

I click the space bar on my computer and Gene Kelly and Debbie Reynolds freeze mid-dance. "Come in."

He steps in, blinks, and flips on my light. Moaning, I close the lid of my laptop and bury my face in the soft purple comforter. Thankfully, my headache has subsided, but now that the show is paused, I'm transported back to a reality in which I made a complete idiot of myself today.

The mattress dips beside me and I can smell Eric's cologne. I have to quiet every muscle in my body that's screaming at me to roll over and cuddle against him.

Definitely not what I need right now.

So I stay put—and surprisingly, so does Eric. He sits there without a word. And that in and of itself is weird. Eric is never quiet. What's going through his mind?

No matter what I'm feeling, I want to be a good friend to him, so I lift my head and shift so I'm lying on my side. He's sitting beside me, a fringed pillow in his lap. His fingers run up and down one of the purple tassels while he frowns.

"What's wrong?"

"Hmm?" He glances up—or rather, down—at me. "Oh. Nothing. Just thinking."

"About …?" I offer a small smile. "What's going on?"

Now that my laptop is muted, I can make out the muffled sound of the television blaring from the living room. And if I know Alexis, the *pop pop pop* is from some sort of shoot-em-up film.

I study Eric some more, wishing I could burrow into his mind, find his thoughts, and bring them out into the light. Despite his last name, he's almost never moody. In fact, his demeanor could normally give Annie (from the self-titled musical) herself a run for her money.

Finally, he looks at me again. "I didn't like how that guy was looking at you today."

"What guy?" It takes me a second. "Wait, Rob? How was he looking at me?"

"I don't know." He shoves the pillow behind his head and lies back to stare up at the ceiling. "It was just shady, that's all. Watch out for him."

"What in the world does that mean?"

"I don't expect you to understand. Just trust me. He's not a good dude."

"Have you heard something about him?" I ask it gently, as if he's a snake about to coil and strike. "Something I should be concerned about?" After all, I'm actually considering taking Rob up on his offer of private voice lessons. But I won't if Eric is getting a bad vibe.

Eric's quiet again.

"Come on. Seriously." I pinch his outside thigh and he swats away my hand. "Please tell me what you're thinking."

"He's into you, Shelby. And I just have a bad feeling about him, all right?"

I blink. "Into *me*?" Shaking my head, I pull myself into a seated position. "He's just being nice. He saw that I was nervous, offered to give me private singing lessons—"

"What?" Eric leaps from the bed and starts pacing my room. He abruptly stops in front of me. "Private lessons? Are you kidding me?"

"He acknowledged how it sounded afterward and assured me he didn't mean anything sketchy."

"Oh, so of course we should believe him. Seriously, Shelbs? You aren't really falling for that, are you?"

My head rears back. "Falling for what?" I fold my arms over my chest. "I told you. He's not into me. "

Eric snorts and mutters something under his breath as he runs his hands through his hair, stopping mid scalp.

What in the world is going on? Maybe he really is concerned for my safety. After all, I'm his best friend. He wants to protect me from bad people. He's always telling me I'm far too trusting—though in the same breath he will say it's something he loves about me.

Or maybe … maybe he's jealous.

Probably not. But … maybe?

It doesn't matter, Shelby Phillips. It. Doesn't. Matter.

Right.

"Hey." I stand and reach for his forearms, tugging his hands from his head. "I won't do the lessons if you are getting a bad vibe. I just thought … well, I could really use the extra practice. Today didn't go so well. And I haven't even sang yet." My lower lip trembles and I inhale a shaky breath, forcing a smile.

He looks at me one, two, three seconds longer, then seems to shake himself loose of whatever trance was holding him captive from his normal jovial self. "Wow. I'm sorry, Shelbs. I just don't want anyone to hurt you. You know that, right?"

"I know."

"You should do the lessons if you want. You're an adult. You have a good head on your shoulders. I don't mean to imply differently." His gaze fixes on my side table and he steps over, reaching for my script, which he holds aloft. "Ready to run lines?"

I breathe out my relief. Things are back to normal. "On one condition."

"Name it."

"Let's order a pizza. I need some fortitude."

"Candy and wine didn't work out so well?" His teasing smile and lifted eyebrows make me laugh.

"Not exactly." My stomach growls in agreement.

Eric bows like he's a stately prince and I'm really a princess. "One pizza and an evening of running lines, coming right up."

"Why, thank you, kind sir."

He starts from the room, then pivots and leans against the doorway. "I'm sorry today was rough, but you really can do this, Shelbs. What I heard sounded great."

And even though he basically knows nothing about theater except what he's absorbed through my tutelage (and countless hours of watching musicals made into movies), the thought warms me enough to trigger a small bit of courage.

I'm going to need a lot more to make it through the next month, but having Eric around nearly twenty-four-seven to buoy my spirits will be just what the doctor ordered.

Yep. Having my best friend under the same roof for such a time as this just might be the gift from above that I didn't know I needed.

five

. . .

I TAKE IT BACK.

I take it allll back.

This is *not* a gift. It's torture. Exquisite torture that feels equally like burning from the inside out and walking barefoot in the snow.

Because while I'm in the middle of waking up the next morning—my mind still fuzzy from lack of coffee—Eric is standing in my kitchen, making eggs.

Shirtless.

I lean heavily against the refrigerator as I take in the sight. His back is to me as he flips the eggs, and with every one of his movements, muscles ripple along his frame. Gripping the handle of the fridge, I remind my fingers that it is NOT their place to trace the straight line of his spine, the ridges of muscle between his shoulder blades, the smooth skin as it tapers to the waistband of his basketball shorts. Still, what I wouldn't give to walk up behind him, wrap my arms around his torso, and lean my head against his back. Maybe even press a kiss right—

"Morning."

I jerk at the word, which is spoken even though his back remains to me. "Um, hi."

How he knows I'm there, I haven't a clue—he just has this uncanny way of seeing me even when I'm trying to be invisible. Kind of like the first time we met.

I was nine, hiding up inside the play structure on the school playground. My one friend, Briana, was absent that day and I didn't know exactly what was going on with my mom ... just that she'd been sick lately.

The world had simply seemed too big and scary that day, so I'd crawled into the hard plastic bubble at the end of one of the climbing tubes on the playground—you know, the kind with scratched-up windows looking out below it? I can't even remember how long I sat there while a few kids climbed in and played with each other, ignoring me. One girl even bumped into me and didn't seem to notice at all.

No one said a word to me.

Until Eric. He was new at school, having just moved in with a different foster family—not that I knew it at the time. I watched him kick at a pile of dirt below. Two girls came up to talk to him, and he shrugged and said something.

Then he glanced up. I ducked my head, unsure if he could really see past the dirty window. I didn't think so. It's one reason I had chosen this place to hide. By the time I got the courage to look again, the girls were alone and giggling. They probably thought he was cute. Not that I could blame them.

I pulled my knees into my chest, set my head down, and

started to hum "Goodnight, My Someone" from The Music Man*—my mom's favorite.*

"That's a nice song."

Stiffening, I peeked up at the voice—and found a pair of kind eyes there. He sat down and asked me what I'd been humming, and slowly drew me out of my shell.

"Shelby."

I blink and realize that Eric has turned. And now I'm caught staring at his chest with what I imagine is a dreamy look in my eyes. Oh, kill me now.

His eyebrows are lifted in amusement and he wiggles the frying pan a bit. "You want some eggs? I can throw a few more on."

I really, really need to look away, but his chest—HIS ABS—are like some sort of drug that render me motionless. *Honestly, Shelby. What is your deal? You've seen him like this a thousand times over the years.*

True. But never *really* like this. In my kitchen. First thing in the morning, before I've had my coffee.

This … this is how it would be if we were together.

Every morning, I could wake up to this sight.

The cool fridge handle has my hand tingling and I finally let go, clearing my throat. "Sorry. Coffee."

He laughs, and the throaty sound has my bare toes curling against the tile. "I brewed a fresh pot just for you."

It really is just for me, because he prefers green smoothies in the morning and Alexis hates even the smell of coffee. "Bless you. And no thanks on the eggs. Not really hungry."

While I move to the hot pink cabinet to snatch a

mug, Eric plates his fried eggs and sits at the table. "Nervous about rehearsal?"

"Yeah." I gnaw on my bottom lip as I lift the coffee pot from the maker and pour in a waterfall of liquid. The nutty aroma fills my lungs and my heart rate slows a bit. "Running lines last night helped though. Thanks again."

"No problem. I told you we'd do whatever it took to get you ready."

He wasn't lying. We spent two hours practicing, and he had me literally rolling on the bed with laughter at his impression of the prince. (I'm actually not sure if he was imitating the prince or Rob playing the prince—but I decided not to ask, since Rob seemed to be a contentious subject.)

I slide into the chair opposite him. "Any word on the apartment situation?" In addition to his clothing, he was able to rescue some family mementos—all he has left of his adoptive parents—from his closet, but everything else was ruined. Thankfully, his renter's insurance will reimburse him, but who knows how long that will take.

"I offer to make the girl some eggs and she's still trying to get rid of me." Eric forks a bite and shoves it into his mouth, then sits back in his chair.

"Stop. You know I love having you here." A little too much, apparently. I rush on. "Just wondering if you'd heard anything more."

Sighing, he takes a sip of his water then shakes his head. "Just that I'm still on the waitlist for the next available apartment. Looks like that will probably happen in a few weeks. So if everything goes according to plan, I'll be out of Lauren's room before she gets back into town."

"Well, see? That worked out perfectly." I fold my hands around my mug, encouraged by its warmth. "Even if it means you have to help me run lines at all hours of the evening."

"I would have done that anyway."

"I know."

His eyes take me in, and the corner of his mouth inches up.

"What?"

Shaking his head, he finishes off his breakfast then stands. "Nothing. I'd better go get dressed." He pauses, turns back to me. "Sorry about this, by the way." He indicates his bare chest. "All of my shirts were dirty so I threw them in the wash early this morning. Should be dry now."

"No worries. I don't mind."

Oh my goodness, I did NOT just say that out loud. But given the way he tilts his head, studying me, I take it that I DID.

I'm sure my cheeks are redder than the one Fourth of July we spent all day on the beach and I forgot my sunscreen. "I just mean, uh, that you should make yourself at home. *Mi casa es su casa* and all that."

Eric chuckles. "I know, Shelbs." Then he gets suddenly serious, a dangerous glint of something unspoken in his eyes. "What else could you possibly have meant?"

Before I can respond, he heads out of the kitchen.

I stare down into my mug, breathe in—one, two, three—release, and take a shaking sip of my coffee. I need to get it together if I'm ever going to survive his stay here. I can't let him see the effect he has on me. Normally, I'm good at hiding it. At least, I think I am. But that's when I see him in smaller doses.

With Eric in every corner of my space, I'm not sure how I'm supposed to keep my secret from him.

But this morning is not for solving that grand question of the universe. It's for rehearsal and dancing and projecting! I chuckle at my inner self's false attempts at enthusiasm while downing the rest of my coffee, scurrying off to my room to get ready, and loading into my Ford Focus to drive to rehearsal.

Eric gives me a pep talk the whole way in the form of a car dance party. At the stoplights, he forces me to do ridiculous moves with him. And if you've never done the shopping cart, the sprinkler, and the Macarena while sitting in a tiny car, you apparently haven't lived (or so Eric says).

An hour later, the entire cast is learning the big dance scene that takes place during the prince's ball. The younger kids are falling all over themselves (and are stinking adorable too) but having fun. The older ones have furrowed brows, concentrating. Several of the middle schoolers flirt in the back row. (Sadly, some of these girls have more game at thirteen than I do at twenty-six.)

Jennifer, the dance teacher here at Redmont Ridge, is

placing people where they should go. Then she turns to Rob and me, settling back on her heels a moment to study us before bouncing forward. Despite her gray hair, Jennifer is far more limber than I am and, truth be told, her ideas seem a bit ambitious for a musical populated by little people. Not to mention the fact we have only four weeks left to perfect this. But this is the least of my worries.

Because tomorrow, we sing. I can't think of that right now, though. Right now, I have a dance to learn.

Jennifer points between us. "Do y'all know how to waltz?"

I nod. In high school, I got mega inspired by Fred Astaire and Ginger Rogers and decided that, even though I would never perform on stage (ha!), I could at least know how to dance. So I begged Eric to take a ballroom dancing class with me at the local community college. He swore me to secrecy even though I told him teasingly that a guy being a good dancer was a total chick magnet.

Rob does the "so-so" movement with his hand. "The basics."

"With your experience? That's astonishing." Clucking her tongue, Jennifer takes hold of Rob's hands and tugs him toward me. His fingers find my waist and my breath hitches—not so much in pleasure as in surprise.

But if Rob *was* flirting with me yesterday (and I still doubt that to be the case), you wouldn't know it today, because his concentration is one thousand percent. He may be holding onto me, but his eyes don't leave Jennifer as she snags a middle school student—a female who clearly knows what she's doing—and gives a mini waltzing demonstration.

She proceeds to show the group more moves. We do our best to mimic her over and over again, slow, then fast, counting the beats—me in my head, Rob out loud.

After several times through, Jennifer calls for attention. "How we doing, leads?"

Rob nods. "I think I've got it."

"Me too," I say.

"Fab. Take it from the top, everyone." Jennifer moves to the side of the stage, and music filters over the speakers.

The notes flow through me. My toes tap and my soul hums. And then, we dance, putting into practice all we've learned. I didn't know how much I'd love this—not just watching it from afar, but being on a stage, being part of the action.

Of course, I'd imagined it. And I remember wondering how it would be when I would sit in the audience at my mom's shows.

But Mom never had a man clinging to her, stepping on her toes, fumbling through the moves and cursing under his breath.

Rob is ... well, he's not the best at dancing. Okay, he's terrible. He's got rhythm—it's not that. He's just so stiff.

Jennifer tells us to take five, and Rob runs a hand down his face. "That was awful, wasn't it?"

I don't want to lie, but I also don't like the idea of discouraging him. "No—"

His pointed look cuts me off.

"Well … maybe just try loosening up a little. You seem really rigid, really anxious. Dancing is just speaking your heart through movement."

"Wow." He stops fretting for a minute, just looks down at me. "I like that. It's really poetic."

And I recognize that look—it's the way my friends' husbands looked at them when they first started dating. How Topher looked at Lauren. Admiration. Interest. And something … more.

Was Eric right? Maybe Rob *does* like me.

"Um, thanks." I wave my hand in the air. "But as I was saying—"

"She's saying you need to lighten up, dude."

And that would be Eric. Rob and I both turn to find my best friend chuckling as he walks onstage. No one else seems to be paying attention to us—they're all scattered and enjoying their break—but sure enough, Eric is here.

He casually slings his arm around my shoulder. "Shelby won't bite. I promise."

Rob's head bobs between us, a wary look on his face. For a moment, no one speaks. Then, "Yeah, I know. I've just never been able to get the hang of dancing. Sounds ridiculous for a guy who's made his career in music, huh?"

His self-deprecation makes me want to give him a hug. "Not at all."

Is it my imagination or does Eric's arm tighten around me?

Probably imagination. Why is he over here, anyway? Not that I am upset, but I haven't seen him since rehearsal began. I look up at him. "Did you need something?"

"I'm here to be of service, actually."

"Oh, yeah?" I smile. "In what way?"

He nudges his chin in Rob's direction. "Thought we could show the prince here how a waltz is supposed to look."

My eyebrows shoot up and something twists in my gut. "What?" Eric wants to dance with me? Here? Now? Why?

We haven't danced together since senior prom, which we clearly went to as friends. When there, he admitted that he hated dancing. So why in the world, after all this time, is he offering to dance with me again?

Maybe I can use his own tactic against him. Humor. Teasing. "You *really* want to get out of painting the set, huh?"

But instead of quirking a grin like he always does, he pivots slightly. The arm that's wrapped around me slides off of my shoulders, his hand catching my arm and coasting all the way down it until he reaches my fingers, which he wraps up in mine. His eyes never leave me.

And all the while, I can't breathe.

Finally, he breaks the spell by pulling his gaze away and placing it on Rob. "I mean, I don't *have* to show you …"

"Oh, actually, I'll take all the help I can get," Rob pipes up. "It would be great to see a man and woman dance. Much as Jennifer and her students know how to dance, it's hard to picture myself in her shoes and remember who is leading who. Please, if you're willing, proceed."

Darn you, Rob. Stay out of things you know nothing about!

Eric turns back to me, lifts a brow. "You up for it?"

I cough. "Yeah, of course."

But there's no "of course" about it. While dancing with Eric probably means nothing to him—I've definitely been imagining the way he's acting since our conversation last night—dancing has been the epitome of true romance to me since I was a preteen. Ever since I sneaked a peek of my dad finding a way to dance with my mom despite the walker she had to use before she was relegated to a wheelchair …

At the memory, I swipe at a tear and Eric's nose scrunches. Before he can ask if I'm okay, I shake my head then place my free hand on his chest, just below where his arm meets his shoulder. He takes our joined hands and extends them, then wraps his free hand around my waist.

We are in position, just like we learned in our class so many years ago. But something is different. Because he's never held me like this. There's something almost possessive, yet somehow still gentle, about the way his hands anchor me. The way his gaze captures mine and won't let go.

And when we start to dance, the moves may be the

same—but the undefinable *something* pulsing between us is new.

New ... and thrilling.

And terrifying.

But I'm imagining it. I have to be. Because nothing has changed between us. We are as we've always been.

As we've got to stay.

six

. . .

TODAY WAS A DISASTER.

Just like that day fourteen years ago, I croaked.

And I do mean, croaked. As in, opened my mouth to sing in front of everyone—and out came a sound reminiscent of the Budweiser frogs.

Mom would be so ashamed. Some legacy I'm living out.

Thankfully, Rob covered for me, coughing and pretending there was something in the air that required all of us to take a water break. I'm sure Sonia saw right through him, but she went ahead and ended rehearsal five minutes early. Afterward, she approached, asked how I was doing with everything.

I wanted to tell her to find someone else. But who would she find on such short notice? Besides, I've been spending every spare moment memorizing the lines so I'm pretty good there.

It's just the singing that needs work.

Which means into the shower I go. It's six in the evening, and Alexis isn't home yet from work—she's still working crazy hours trying to perfect her pitch. Eric is gone too, out grabbing us something for dinner, which means I have some time to work on my songs before risking anyone hearing me.

I rustle through my dresser, grab a T-shirt and soft pajama shorts, and scurry down the quiet hallway to the bathroom. It's so different living here now, with Evie and Kayla gone. The house was always so lively, and Lauren and I shared a room. I admit that my introverted self loves having my own space to retreat to now, but there's also something kind of sad about the stillness.

When I'm in the bathroom, I shut and lock the door, disrobe, flick on the water, and wait for the stream to heat up. Mom's locket swings forward as I lean against the counter and study myself in the mirror.

Pale eyes, pale skin, pale hair—I am no great beauty. And I've always been fairly okay with that. Beautiful girls like my friends attract a lot of attention, and I hate having all eyes on me. All eyes on me means it would be easier for people to find me lacking.

So, yeah. Okay with blending in. Besides, beauty is fleeting. With Mom, I saw how her own physical beauty faded in her last years—but her kindness, her thoughts for others, only grew.

And that made her more beautiful than anything.

I peer into the mirror, into my own eyes, and I pray to see her—a brave warrior fighting against something daunting—even just a little bit in me.

If she can do battle against her disease, against the

unknown, surely I can take on my fear of singing in front of others. (And of other things too, like the idea of living forever without telling Eric how I feel about him. But one thing at a time.)

"Send me some strength, please."

After the prayer is uttered, I step into the shower. The water is a gentle rainfall around me and I let it soak my hair. Let it caress me and whisper to my soul. Let it soothe me into its rhythm so that I can sing.

It starts low within me, a bit scratchy at first. But then, the fear melts away and I just remember those moments with Mom toward the end of her life, when she called me her songbird. When I sang her lullabies and stroked her hair.

And now, as I wash my own—as I cleanse my body from the fear of performing for other people—I sing for her again.

I sing for *me*.

The water seems to be coming harder now, pounding in time with the beat of my heart, which is soaring. Because I haven't sang like this in a very long time.

But can I do it when others are listening? Maybe I'm not actually any good. Maybe it just *feels* good. Maybe Sonia didn't hear correctly. Maybe she was simply desperate for someone, anyone, and I was the only option.

I turn off the water, grab my towel, and quickly dry off before getting dressed. Then I open the door—and yelp.

Because Eric's leaning against the opposite door-jamb, the one that leads into Lauren's room. His room, for now. And the look on his face is pure awe mixed with something else. Something I can't quite define.

For a long beat, he just stares at me. I swallow hard at his perusal and lean against the wall.

"Shelby, I had no idea you were so amazing." He straightens, takes a step toward me. "That was next level."

I'm definitely about to die due to embarrassment. But also, the sweetness of the moment, the way Eric is supporting me like he always does. "Thanks," I manage. The light from the living room shines into the hallway, which has grown darker since I entered the bathroom. How long was I in there? "What time is it? Did you get dinner?"

"Don't change the subject, Shelbs. You need to march on that stage at rehearsal tomorrow and sing like that. You're gonna stop everyone in their tracks and have everyone's attention."

"Just what I love. A million eyes on me." I offer a small smile to show him I'm jesting—though of course there's a grain of truth in every joke.

"I know you hate attention." He takes another step. "But what are you so afraid of? There's the usual stage fright, but this fear seems to go deeper."

I tuck my hands behind me and press them flat against the wall. "You know why." Haven't I ever told him about what happened that day?

"I know your mom died, and obviously the grief tore you apart." Eric says this softly as he reaches for the hem of my light green shirt and runs his thumb along it.

I hold back a shiver at his nearness. He does this

often, getting close to me, but I don't think he knows the effect he has. "And you were there to put me back together again."

"You did the same for me through all the ups and downs." Eric licks his lips, and his gaze drifts up to catch mine again. "But there's more, isn't there? Did something else happen?"

"The audition."

His forehead wrinkles. "What audition?"

"Six months after Mom died. Seventh grade?"

"I don't know what you're talking about."

"I really never told you?"

He shakes his head.

I inhale a trembling breath, and with the pure oxygen comes once again the scent that is all Eric—a mixture of his citrusy cologne plus clean and crisp soap. "I decided to try out for the musical that year. I wanted to feel close to Mom again and I thought that maybe …"

Biting my lip, I tilt my head back and look at the ceiling. It's lower than the ceiling in the bedrooms and living room, and for a moment, I am caged. But then I remember the freedom of expressing myself in the shower. Even if no one was listening (or so I thought), maybe Mom was. Her strength wends through me now. "Anyway, I got up on the stage to sing and basically what happened earlier today happened then. I opened my mouth and the most awful sound came out. Like something dying. Well, not just something. It was—it was the sound of my *voice* dying."

"But not your physical voice."

Somehow, he just gets me. He just knows. "No, not my physical voice." I wait a moment. "The something inside of me that wanted to speak. That maybe kind of wanted to be seen. I think it died with Mom. My *song* died with Mom."

"But it didn't, Shelbs."

At the soft timbre of his voice, I bring my gaze down again. And he's close. So close.

Eric lifts his hand and presses a wet strand of my hair behind my ear. "You may have tried to bury your voice, but it has shone through in everything you do. You have such a light, and I'm not just talking about singing. You're always taking the backstage to others, letting them have the spotlight." Then my best friend leans in closer—so close I can feel his warm breath on my lips. "But don't you know you're the brightest star of them all?"

I'd smile at the sweet picture he's painting if my heart wasn't about to leap out of my chest at his nearness. "Th-that's not how I see it."

"I know." Eric plays with my earlobe. "And that's what makes you so great."

My pulse is going haywire, and thank goodness I'm leaning against the wall, because I'm sinking. Drowning in the something that looks an awful lot like adoration in Eric's eyes.

And all it would take to show him how I feel is to lean forward a fraction of an inch.

Just a tiny, itty bitty, minuscule fraction …

"Hey, guys—oh. Um. Am I interrupting something?"

Eric steps backward and runs a hand through his hair, super casual as if we hadn't been caught nearly …

I straighten, push myself off the wall, and squint into the light of the living room, where Alexis stands, arms crossed, an orange eyebrow raised in amusement.

"What? No. We were just … talking," I say.

"Yep. And now, it's time to eat." Eric strides past Alexis toward the kitchen.

I start to follow, and Alexis's stare tells me everything I need to know.

That it's possible the cat is finally out of the bag—and I don't know if I can force it back in without getting scratched to death.

Because if they haven't picked up on my unintentional broadcast of feelings, then they're completely blind.

seven

. . .

I'VE NEVER UNDERSTOOD the acronym TGIF more than I do today.

Because I DO thank goodness it's Friday. I've got nearly a week of rehearsals under my belt. Know most of my lines. Am getting proficient with the dances.

And today, in front of everyone, I sang.

Sure, it was a duet—not one of my solo numbers—and that had to have helped, to know I wasn't alone up there. And Rob did take me aside afterward and give me a few pointers for projecting.

But overall … it went pretty well.

And so much of that was because I kept hearing Eric's voice in my head. *"Don't you know you're the brightest star of them all?"* It made me want to shine, to make Mom proud, to show all of my students—those adorable kids—that hard things are possible.

I've got a ways to go before I'll be comfortable with the music, and the thought of singing for a crowd on opening night in a little less than a month makes me want to vomit. But I'm getting there. Forward motion and all that.

Progress is—

"All right. Spill it."

Yelping, I yank my water glass away from the refrigerator—and proceed to splash it all over the kitchen floor.

I turn to Alexis. "I'm guessing that's not what you meant."

"Not quite." Alexis, who has now snuck up on me for the second time in two days, strides into the kitchen, snatches a towel from the sink, and pushes it into my free hand. "Guessing you know what I *did* mean, though."

Ugh. Yes.

I've successfully avoided talking with my friend one on one since she discovered Eric and me almost kissing in the hallway last night. (We *did* almost kiss, right? I didn't imagine it? I'm not sure how I could have. I've watched enough romantic movies and musicals to know an almost kiss when I see one—even though I've never been the one on the ALMOST receiving end of one.)

But Alexis wasn't the only one I avoided the last twenty-four hours. I made up an excuse to ride alone to rehearsal today. Eric shrugged and said, "Cool," acting like those moments in the hallway last night didn't mean anything. And that's for the best.

It is.

I set my now half-filled glass on the counter and squat

to clean up the mess on the tile. It's not super easy to do in a skirt and heels, but we're about to head out for a girls' night at a local restaurant and I felt like dressing up.

"Well?" Alexis tugs her lime green ponytail over her shoulder and starts to braid it.

"Yes, I know what you meant."

"And?"

Using the counter as leverage, I hoist myself upright. The lining of my heels digs into the tops of my toes. "And, there's nothing to spill."

"Isn't there, though?" Alexis ties off her braid and flips it back over her shoulder. It swings like a pendulum behind her back for a few seconds before stopping.

Sighing, I move to the window on the other side of the kitchen and look out. The trees in our small backyard block the setting sun. "Nothing can happen, Alexis."

"But you finally, at long last, admit that you *want* something to."

I lick my lips. There's no use in lying about it. To my friend. To myself. "Yeah."

"You love him."

My heart squeezes at the truth laid bare, out in the world for the second time since my sister spoke it aloud. Is it completely obvious to everyone else? Instead of replying with words, I simply nod.

And start to cry.

Not one to give hugs, Alexis sidles up beside me at the counter. "For what it's worth, he loves you too."

"What? No." Maybe there's attraction there, but love? "He's never said so."

"Well, neither have you, and yet we all know it."

Great. "Who is *we all*?"

"Our group of friends. Their men. Basically anyone who has seen you together. We've all wondered when the two of you were going to finally make something happen." Alexis bumps me with her hip. "Honestly, I'm wondering what I would have come home to if I'd been a few minutes later last night."

I know she's teasing me, but I just … can't. I move away from her, walk down the hallway, into the bathroom, where I grab a tissue off the back of the toilet and dab my eyes. The tissue comes away stained black with mascara.

A shadow fills the doorway. "I didn't mean to make you cry."

"You didn't."

She huffs a laugh. "Okay. Sure." Then she sobers, cocks her head. "So you've really never told him how you feel?"

"I … I can't."

"Why not?"

I bite my lip and turn to face her, then sit back against the counter. The cool surface seeps through my thin skirt to my skin. Should I tell my friend? I know Eric won't overhear—he's gone for the evening to hang out with Connor and Josh while their wives join Alexis and me. So what's the harm?

If anyone will understand my hesitancy to be in a relationship, it's Alexis. I don't exactly know what happened to make her so jaded about the male species, but I do know it'll take a miracle—some sort of crazy amazing story—for her to be open to love for herself. So I'm ninety-five percent sure that *she's* not going to push me toward being with Eric.

Because that's definitely *not* what I need right now. I need someone to talk straight with me. To remind me why being with him is indeed a terrible idea.

So I tell her everything. My and Eric's past. The genetic test. Why we can't be together.

When I'm done, my body heaves a sigh of relief and I sink to the bathroom floor. Alexis lowers herself too, sitting against the door frame. She folds her legs up into her chest, blinks. Seems to consider what to say.

But what is there to say? I've come up with the only possible solution.

Finally, "You know, Shelby … you spend so much time worrying about other people. But your happiness matters just as much as Eric's. And I'm willing to bet he'd say so too—if you gave him the chance. The choice."

Okay, that was sooooo not what I thought she'd say.

"I …" How do I respond? How do I explain? "Don't you see? If I tell him how I feel, there are only two ways this can play out. One: We date and break up and I lose my best friend. Or two: We fall in love, get married, and he resents me forever for stealing his dream of having biological children."

"There are lots of ways to make a family."

Man, it's like Deb and Alexis got together and concocted a plan to beat me over the head with the exact same phrases. "Of course there are. I'm very open to adoption myself."

"And how do you know he's not? Did he actually say he wanted *biological* children? Or just that he wants a family of his own?"

"Both."

My mind wanders back to that night. *My family had a huge trampoline and he and I had spent the evening jumping like we were young again. Eric showed off with some backflips while I applauded him for his efforts.*

But after a while, we settled down, lying back on the trampoline, side by side. My heart had felt stirrings for him before this, but I knew he didn't see me that way. So even though I wished he'd grab my hand, I contented myself with being near him, surrounded by his teenage essence of ocean spray body wash and a hint of sweat—which on him, somehow never smelled bad. His scent was masculine, sweet. All Eric.

The sky was clear, the air crisping up, and he pointed out several constellations he'd learned in astronomy. I teased him about how well he'd paid attention, considering his track record of sleeping in a few classes.

He laughed. "It helps that Sherise Donovan is in there."

My heart folded in on itself. I forced a giggle, nudging him with my shoulder. "That explains so much."

We both quieted after that, just watching the great expanse before us. I wondered if Mom could see us, if there really were holes in the floor of Heaven like that old song said.

And just like that, a star skittered across the sky and I knew it was true—knew she was watching over me. A tear leaked from my eye as I pointed. "Eric, look. Quick."

Then he did take my hand, squeezed. "Make a wish, Shelbs."

So I did.

He let go, then turned his face to me, our noses inches apart. "I know we're not supposed to tell, but … what did you wish for?"

I breathed him in, holding back the rest of my tears. "For just one more song. One more moment."

Despite the darkness, I felt his understanding. "With your mom?"

I nodded, and he gathered me into a hug, held me against his chest. After a few blissful moments there, I pulled back. "And you? What did you wish for?"

His gaze lingered on the stars. "I want to know more about my family. Not my adoptive family—my biological one. Maybe find them one day."

"You should. I'll help, if you want."

"Thanks." He squeezed my shoulders again and a deep breath left his body. "It sounds so dumb, but I guess I'm afraid I'll always be alone in the world."

"You'll never be alone. My family loves you." And so did I.

"I know, and I love them too. But like, I don't belong to you guys."

"That's not true. You do, and you always will."

"You're right." Eric sighed. "I know it's not blood alone that makes people a family, but what if I never have another person in this world who shares my blood? That matters too, Shelbs."

I wanted to cry for him, for the little boy I'd known who had played off his pain with humor, deflected the deepest wounds of his past. He never talked about them, but I knew they were there. And I only wanted to help cheer him up. Give him hope. "You'll find them."

He shrugged. "Maybe. I know almost nothing about them except that my bio mom died, so it doesn't seem all that possible."

Another thought came to me. "Well. Even if you don't find your bio family, you could have kids someday. Carry on your bloodline that way. Make your own family." I didn't dare wish that it would be with me. If I put that wish out there into the universe, I'd only be disappointed. I'd seen the kinds of girls Eric dated, and I was the farthest thing from them.

"Yeah, I guess that's true." He nodded, and a smile crept across his lips. "Okay, that settles it. I'm amending my wish. Or, expanding on it, I guess."

"Can you do that after the star has already passed?" I teased.

"Sure I can, so long as you don't tell."

"My lips are sealed."

"Are you positive you're remembering it correctly? It was like a decade ago." Alexis's voice brings me back to reality.

I startle, blink. "I remember every detail. He wants to have someone in his life he's actually related to. It's his greatest dream, and I can't deprive him of it."

"And what about *your* greatest dream?"

"I have dreams beyond marrying Eric."

"Of course you do. But it doesn't take a genius to know that one of your greatest dreams is to have a marriage like your parents did. To raise a whole bunch of kids, just like your family did. And to make sure that each person in your care feels loved for who they are."

My eyes widen at my friend's assessment. I had no idea she was so observant. But that's Alexis for you—keeping everything close to the vest.

She seems to take in my surprise and her lips quirk up on one side as she stands and offers me a hand. "Come on. Food and friends will make you feel better."

I let her hoist me to my feet then turn and make sure I don't look like a raccoon. After another quick swipe under my eyes, I toss the tissue into the trash. "Thanks, Lexi Lou."

She rolls her eyes. "I thought I'd get a reprieve from that awful nickname while Lauren was gone."

Before she can leave, I snatch her into a hug. "Seriously. Thanks."

She's stiff at first but eventually relaxes before pulling away. "You're gonna figure this out. Maybe our friends can help."

"Oh no." I shake my head so quick my dangling rosebud earrings smack my neck. "You can't say a word about this to them."

Without another word, Alexis turns on her heels and hurries down the hallway toward the door—and I'm left wondering if she heard me.

An hour later, after fighting Friday evening traffic, we end up at a cute Italian restaurant on the bay. Kayla made reservations, so we're able to bypass the line as the hostess leads us out to a deck situated right on the water. Evie and Kayla sit at a wooden table covered in a red and white checked tablecloth. Soft music joins the cadence of the ocean, giving the entire place a warm ambiance despite the nip in the air. Lights are strung overhead and every seat is filled except the two beside our friends.

Evie sees us first and waves from behind her menu, which is nearly as large as her head. Tonight, she's hunkered down in one of her frumpy librarian sweaters, as she likes to call them. Once, Kayla tried to get rid of them all, but Evie still has a few holdouts.

"Finally," is all Kayla says as we slip into our seats. "I'm starving and I've already eaten all the free bread."

"What, you're not going to weep at the sight of your beautiful friends?" Alexis teases, no doubt remembering our last interaction with a very tearful Kayla.

Kayla flashes her an "I'm not amused" glare. "I told you. Emotions are up and down. Tonight you get cranky Kayla."

"Joy. So back to normal then?"

I wince at Alexis's barb. Because, however much she jests, sometimes the woman does not have a filter, and neither does Kayla. And they both have iron wills. So when the two of them go at it … well, it's not pretty.

Evie and I exchange a look, one that tells me at least she and I are on the same page. Time to change the subject. "Were we still planning to call Lauren after dinner?"

"Why wait?" Evie reaches into her bag and pulls out her phone.

"Uh, because it might be rude?" Alexis says. "We're not exactly the only ones here."

"Oh, you're one to talk about being rude," Kayla mutters.

We need to get more food into the pregnant lady, stat. But in the meantime, a distraction will do. I give Evie a nod. "Let's do it."

Evie dials and turns her volume up, and I'm just praying the dining patrons around us will forgive our obvious lack of decorum.

When Lauren's face pops up on the screen, a fierce pang of longing hits me. I've missed this—just the five of us. And I can't wait for her to return. She's supposed to be back just before my show and promised to be there opening night.

"Ladies!" Her shrill voice carries over the airwaves and punctuates the calm.

We all say hello, except Kayla who is busy scrounging in her purse for something. When she finds a protein bar, she pumps her fist and waves at Lauren.

"We didn't wake you, did we?" I ask.

"Nah. Though it is past midnight here. But I couldn't sleep anyway, so this is perfect. Today Topher took me on a drive through the countryside and it's so gorgeous and oh man, I just love this place. And that man." She sighs and leans back against a fancy silver puffed headboard. Her brown hair is piled in a bun at the top of her head.

"Aw, that's so sweet." Evie fiddles with her wedding ring. She and Connor got married last December at the Japanese Friendship Garden. It seems both forever ago and just yesterday.

"Where are y'all?" Lauren squints.

"Out to dinner."

"Oh. That explains the woman hovering behind all of you, waiting for you to notice her."

Oops. We all swivel in our seats to find a twenty-something with a subtly pierced nose standing there with a pad of paper and pen. "Hi, I'm your server tonight. Gwen." She eyes the phone and her nose wrinkles slightly. "Can I get you something to drink?"

Normally, most of us would order an alcoholic beverage, but since Evie and Kay can't drink, I don't want them to feel left out, which means it's water with lime for me. Alexis has no such reservation and orders a bellini. The server takes yet another look at the phone—where Lauren waits quietly—and lets loose a barely discernible huff before leaving to fulfill our drink order.

We all turn back to face Lauren again. "Well, she looked less than thrilled by my presence, so maybe y'all should call me back after dinner. I'll be up, I'm sure."

"That sounds like a good plan," I say, because I really don't want to face the passive-aggressive wrath of Gwen again.

"First, we have an important order of business." Alexis looks directly at me.

No. She wouldn't.

A glint of determined mischief flashes in her eyes.

Oh no. She would. She will.

"Alexis …" My tone and my eyes beg her to stay quiet.

But she only shakes her head. "It's for your own good, Shelby."

"What is?" Kayla places her half-eaten protein bar on the table and leans forward.

"Yeah, what's going on?" Lauren's voice comes out louder than it's been, which has Evie yanking the phone slightly away from herself.

I glance around and find several other diners staring at us. Then, to my friends, "Guys, please. Let's talk about this later."

"You'll only try to avoid us if we do that, Shelby." Alexis gives her attention to everyone else. "Shelby and Eric practically made out last night."

"What?" Lauren's shriek could break glass. I wouldn't be surprised if Topher came running from the other end of the palace to find out what was wrong.

As for Evie and Kayla, they're both just staring at me, eyes wide.

Then Kayla starts to cackle. "Finally! At long last! Evs, you owe me twenty bucks."

"You bet on this?" I can't help the hurt in my tone. This isn't a game. It's my life.

My friends must be able to hear it too, because Kayla immediately shrinks in her seat and starts to sniffle. "I'm sorry, Shelby. You're right. I shouldn't have done that." She reaches over and squeezes my hand. "But we're so happy. You guys are perfect for each other.

We've known it for a long time. We're just glad you realized it too."

"Uh, is the connection bad or am I the only one who is asking for deets?" Laurens says. "Details, details, Miss Shelby! And now."

And it's all I can do not to grab my menu and use it as a shield to hide behind. Thank goodness Gwen decides to show back up with our drinks and to take our dinner orders, so I have a few minutes to gather my wits.

To remember that these are my friends. They want my best. They really do.

And maybe, just maybe, they have advice for me. After all, three are in wonderful relationships.

Not that that's in the cards for me. At least, no way that I can see.

But … what if there *was* a path, one that I'm just not seeing because I'm too close to the situation? Honestly, I have nothing to lose at this point. So, once Gwen leaves, I tell my friends everything.

When I'm finished, the silence is palpable, invaded only by the noises surrounding us. But we are a five-person bubble and, crazy as it sounds, I can feel my friends' love for me in that space.

"Wow," Kayla sniffles again and blows her nose. "I had no idea you were carrying that load."

"Same here," Lauren says, her voice hushed. "But we're here to help you carry it."

My lips tremble and I blink back the tears. At the table next to us, a family with children sits down, but not even the youngest boy's crying over his tablet being put away can dim this moment. "Thanks, guys."

Evie looks from one person to the next before her eyes finally settle on me. "I'm so sorry for everything you've been through, friend. It's a lot." And I know, as someone who also lost a loved one as a child, she understands. "Now, what to do about Eric …"

Stuffing her tissue into her fist, Kayla points at me. "I say you just go for it. Lay a kiss on him that he'll never forget and see what happens."

Alexis rolls her eyes. "And this from the dating coach. That's always your advice. *Go kiss him.*" Her mimic of Kayla's voice is spot on. "Does anyone actually *do* that?"

"Hey! My methods work. Just ask the eighty-five percent of my clients whose relationships have worked out."

"And what about the other fifteen?" Alexis shoots back. "Do they have to go into hiding from embarrassment?"

"Hey, now." Kayla taps the side of her nose. "Maybe you should let me find *you* a nice guy, Alexis. You wouldn't be criticizing me then."

"I'd rather poke my eyes out with this fork, thanks." Alexis's face has reddened significantly, matching her jacket.

Kayla tsks. "What about that Dax guy at your w—"

"Shelby," Evie interrupts before Mount St. Alexis can erupt. Then she takes my hand in hers. "My best advice is to be honest with Eric. I know it's not simple, but tell him how you feel. Then you can have a conversation and figure out what it is you both want. And I really don't think you need to worry that Eric won't return your feelings."

They're kind to say that, but of course I can't be sure of anything until I hear from him that I am what he wants. "But even if he does, and I tell him about my decision not to have kids, what happens if he says he doesn't care—but I know he does? I can't do that to him. Relationships require sacrifice."

I know it at the core of my being because it's something my mother drilled into all of us. Sacrifice equals love. And it's hard, because sacrifice in turn requires bravery. And I don't feel all that brave.

"There's sacrifice and then there's pretending you know what's best for someone else." Alexis takes a sip of her bellini.

When Kayla glares at her, she lifts both hands. "What? It's true. Until she gives Eric a say in the matter, she doesn't even know if she *needs* to sacrifice. Maybe he's changed his mind about what he wants. Maybe she's depriving herself for no reason."

"It isn't for no reason. I don't want to be selfish."

"No one who knows you would call you selfish, hon." Lauren's sweet words shoot across the Atlantic and wrap themselves around my heart.

Are my friends right? Am I just pretending I know what's best? That would actually be prideful, not selfless.

Oy. My head hurts. "I don't know what to do."

"I've got it." Evie snaps her fingers. "What about a DNA test?"

"She already did one of those, remember?" Kayla says.

"Not her. Eric. What if Eric did a DNA test? So many people are doing them now, trying to find relatives they didn't know before. Do you think you could get him to do one?"

I'm still not fully following, but given all the emotional energy I've drained this week—between the show and the Eric situation—that's not surprising. "He actually did one years ago but didn't get any results that I know of. But what does that …"

Oh. Wait a minute.

If Eric could find his biological family—someone he's related to—AND he wanted to give a relationship with me a shot, we could both have what we want. "That could work."

And I realize there are a lot of "ifs" in that scenario.

But even one "if" gives me more hope than I've had in the last eight years. It's a life preserver and it's floating, bobbing, far away.

But I'm a drowning woman. And right now, I'm willing to swim hard toward any speck of life on the horizon.

eight

· · ·

TRADITIONS MEANT everything to my mother. And they mean everything to me. There's nothing like a tradition to show someone they mean something special to you.

And that's why every July 16, rain or shine, weekday or weekend, I find myself here, at the San Diego Zoo.

Because this place holds so many beautiful memories for me.

It's where my dad proposed to my mom so many years ago on the SkyFari aerial tram as they soared over the grounds.

Where my family had season passes and went every break from school, as well as random days my mom would take us out to experience the park with fewer tourists.

Where each of us kids had at least one birthday party—mine when I turned seven, a "big age" according to Mom. Of course, every birthday was a big age for her. Every year was worth celebrating.

And even though it's hard to celebrate another birthday without her here, I know this is exactly where she'd be if she was still alive. So here I am too, and Eric beside me.

We approach the hippo enclosure and take the walkway down and out of the sun. It's not all that hot today—the normal high seventies of summer—but the sky is mostly clear and the sun is strong today. We've been here since the zoo opened a few hours ago, and unsurprisingly, the crowds have begun to swell. But together we've already covered lots of ground, seeing many of the most popular animals—giraffes, elephants, bears, and the like—and sharing fun memories of Mom and my family along the way.

I don't remember when we started doing this as a tradition, but it's a given every year without fail. Sonia wasn't happy when I begged off rehearsal and I almost gave in, but Eric backed me up and reminded me of how important this day is to me.

And I'm so glad I listened.

After a few minutes of waiting for a family with eight children to vacate the clear plexiglass separating the viewing platform from the water where the hippos are swimming, we finally step forward. The water is a bit murky, filled with floating bits of grass and bubbles. But there, swimming toward us, comes a hippo.

"Oh my goodness, look!" I point out the baby following her mom. The sight squeezes my throat.

Eric leans in. "I can't see anything."

"That's because you have your sunglasses on." I poke him in the ribs because his smile tells me he knows it.

"Ah! You're right." He takes his sunglasses off and blinks. "Much better."

Things have been back to normal for us all week. I don't know whether to be thankful or a little bit sad that he hasn't brought up what I'm secretly dubbing "The Hallway Incident." Could be I'm thinking about it in different terms than he is. Perhaps it really didn't affect him like it did me.

But the memory of that spine-tingling moment has me thinking long and hard about doing what Evie suggested eight days ago at the restaurant. How does one go about randomly bringing up a DNA test, though? I'm hoping it will come naturally if it's supposed to. But that doesn't stop my palms from sweating and my stomach from heating at the thought.

"Hey, little dude," Eric says, apparently to the baby hippo, who swims past us and turns for another lap around the pool. On his heels comes a much larger hippo, maybe his dad. "You know"—Eric leans closer to me—"hippos are the world's deadliest animal."

"Oh, really?" I just smile, because this is our game. He tells me random things about each animal we see and I pretend like he hasn't repeated the same fact year after year.

"Mmm hmm. They kill more people than lions do because even though they're herbivores, they attack when threatened." Eric moves slightly behind me to make room for some older kids who want a closer look.

"Fascinating," I murmur, still smiling. The giant beast comes so close to the viewing window that I can see the stumpy whiskers on his snout, such a contrast to the smooth and mostly hairless skin on the rest of his body. His eye seems to catch mine.

"Watch out!" Eric's hands dart out to either of my sides, tickling the sensitive spots just above my waist.

I jump and my heart leaps with the rest of my body as I spin and smack him on the chest. "Eric!"

He's laughing, clutching his stomach. "Your face."

The kids around us laugh with him, their parents too. I fake a chuckle and hightail it toward the exit, emerging into the bright sunlight again.

"Shelbs, wait." Eric jogs to catch me. "Are you mad at me?"

"No." And I'm not. Not really. "I just …"

"Hate being the center of attention. I know. I'm an idiot. I'm sorry." And his contrite eyes tell me he is. "I didn't mean to embarrass you."

The thing is … huh. "I'm actually not quite as upset as I usually would be."

"Really?"

"Yeah." How weird. Normally, if a group of people were to laugh at me, I'd be shaking, on the verge of tears —reliving that moment fourteen years ago on stage when I couldn't sing and people pointed and jeered. "I mean, obviously I didn't want to stay there a second longer, but look." I hold out my hand and it's steady.

"Maybe doing the show is actually giving you some of your confidence back. This week has seemed to go really well."

He's right. It has. I finally feel like I'm starting to get the hang of it. "Thanks to your excellent line reading skills." He's helped me more than once to memorize my lines, to practice my blocking on stage.

"How very true." Eric slips on his sunglasses and adjusts his blue Padres hat, which is sitting backward on his head. "But I still feel bad about scaring you. Let me make it up to you."

Before I can protest, he's tugging me down the trail. We're surrounded by a gorgeous assortment of ficus, eucalyptus, acacia, and bamboo trees that have likely stood in this very place for generations. Birds chatter in the trees and in the distance, tigers roar and monkeys screech as we descend toward the park's entrance. "Where are we going?"

"You'll see. It's my treat this year."

And then I know. The sky tram. "But we always save that until the end."

"Traditions are good. But sometimes change is good too."

A low-hanging tree branch nearly smacks me in the face as he practically drags me toward the front. Eric's words are a reminder of the choices I have before me—to stay here, in the comfortable and familiar, or to venture forward into the unknown.

What if change *could* be the best thing for us? Could it be better than this—racing through a place I love with the man I love, a man I know I will have forever as a friend? Who will back me up no matter what? Who sees me and knows me without my having to say a word?

And yet, the irony—in order to have what my heart

truly longs for, I *have* to say a word. A lot of words. And I am not a wordsmith by any means.

Finally, we arrive at the sky tram and the line is actually not too bad. After we buy tickets and wait for a few minutes, we climb into the blue bucket seat with a bench and sit beside each other. There are no straps or buckles, but the railing comes above our shoulders, so I feel secure tucked away in here with Eric.

The tram creaks and moves and we are off on a twenty-minute ride through the sky.

For the first few minutes, we point out the animals we see below, but then I just settle into my seat. Eric's arm is around the back of the bench—effectively around my back too, though not in a romantic way. A breeze cools my cheeks and peace washes over me. "Can you believe that Dad proposed to my mom in this very airspace?"

"It's pretty special if you think about it. We could be sitting in the exact same seat they did once upon a time."

"Maybe." Wouldn't that be something?

"I wish I'd had more years with her." Eric's voice is calm, reverent.

"Me too." I brush a tear from my cheek. "She really loved you. *That boy lights up the room with laughter wherever he goes.* That's what she'd say."

"That boy had no one until your family came along." He shifts in the seat and pulls his hands back into his lap, placing each palm flat on top of a knee. "And I'd never want to do anything to jeopardize my relationship with them."

That's a strange thing to say. "That would never happen. I think my family likes you more than they like me." Not that I blame them. Who wouldn't love the fun-loving, goofy guy that he is?

"Well, that's not accurate." There's something tight in his tone, something that makes me sit back a bit, turn in the seat so I can see him better. "Your brothers in particular would cast me aside in a second if I ever did something stupid."

What is he even talking about? My brothers practically worship the ground he walks on. To them, he's just another Phillips sibling. A first pick for the football games. Someone to heckle. "Stupid like what?"

"Like hurting you."

I laugh, because that's ridiculous. "You're my best friend. You'd never hurt me."

"Tell that to Cody."

"Cody?" Cody and I are closest in age, but he's still four years older than me. "What did he do?"

Eric doesn't say anything for a long moment. The wind whistles past us, rocking our bucket ever so slightly. Then, "Remember when I took you to senior prom?"

"Yeah."

Even though we went as best friends, I thought maybe he liked me as more. He'd even kind of flirted with me in the few days leading up to it. But when I came down the stairs at my house in my dress—a strapless pale pink gown that shimmered in the light—he looked right through me, as if, for the first time, he *didn't* see me.

And when we danced, he held me stiff. Nearly a foot apart. And we slow danced to exactly two songs, and that was because I begged him. It seemed like his good nature and indulgences only went so far.

After that, any pretense of flirtation, any hopes I had that we might be together eventually, fizzled. And then, a few months later, I got the results of my genetic test and those hopes died completely. We went back to being just best friends. Which is probably all we ever were in reality. It was just my mind messing with me.

What could he possibly have to say about prom?

"Well, when I got there, Cody answered the door. He was back visiting from college, I think. Anyway, he took one look at me, hauled me inside, and told me in no uncertain terms that I'd better be careful."

"Careful about what?"

He inhales a sharp breath. "Careful not to mess things up with you. I guess he thought we were going as a couple."

My stomach twists, and it has nothing to do with the view or the fact the solid ground is so far below me. "But you assured him we were just friends, right?"

"Yeah, I did." He trails off. "But if I'm honest, I *wasn't* just your friend."

My gaze shoots to him. I can't see his eyes behind his sunglasses, but his shoulders are relaxed. There's no sign that he's tense despite the bomb he just dropped. "What do you mean?"

He shrugs, glances away. Behind him there's a puff of clouds trying to block out the sun, but I can still see everything I need to. The slight crease in his forehead, the small pucker of his lips. "I really liked you back then, Shelby—and not as a brother or a friend would."

I suck in air. "What?"

"Yeah. Why do you think I told you I didn't like dancing at prom? I couldn't stand holding you without having you, that's why."

I'd always wondered about that declaration. It had seemed to come out of the blue. But ... "You never said anything. About liking me, I mean."

"I knew I wasn't good enough for you." At my protesting squeak, he grabs my hand and squeezes, facing me once again. "I was just a foster kid with no prospects, nothing but a joke in his back pocket and dreams that weren't amounting to much."

"But you made something of yourself. Worked your way through school. There's nothing 'not good enough' about you." How could he even think that about himself? Doesn't he know that he is—he always was—a thousand times better than any other guy I could be with?

He shakes his head, smiling. "And a lot of that is because of you. Because of your family and what they've given me. But Cody made it really clear that if I messed things up with you, that if I hurt you—intentionally or not—I'd have no place with your family anymore. And your family has been the only constant in my life. Besides convincing myself that you didn't feel more for me than friendship, I decided that I couldn't stand to lose them." He laughs, but there's self-deprecation in it. "That probably sounds really pathetic, huh?"

"Not pathetic. Sweet." I bump his shoulder with my

own, my mind racing with all that there is to unpack from what he just told me. "Cody was right. You're part of the family." And, oh wow, this is the perfect opportunity. I inhale all the courage imbued in me last week with my friends and reach for that metaphorical life preserver. "But what about your biological family? Did you ever hear anything from the DNA test you took a while back? Any matches?"

He lowers his sunglasses and wrinkles his nose. "Where did that thought come from? You sick of sharing your family with me?" His voice teases but I sense a real question in there.

Clearly, I do not possess the kind of stealth this mission requires. If I could be outright honest with him, I would. But I'm scared. Scared the life preserver will spring a leak. That I'll lose this man, not just as a potential forever love, but as a friend too. And from what I'm hearing, a relationship between us holds risk for him too. He'd lose my family—or so he thinks, anyway.

Plus, he's declared that he used to have feelings for me, not that he currently does.

"What's mine is yours, Eric. I've always been happy to share. I-I just know you had hoped at one time to connect with a relative."

He shrugs. "After so many dead ends, I shut down my account. Decided to be content with what I had. And I am."

But his look pierces me, and there's a longing in it. For what, though? For a blood family? Or ... maybe he's really *not* content with the current status of our relationship. Maybe, like me, he wants more but is afraid to say anything. It's on the tip of my tongue, this desire to push myself over the edge, to finally give in, ask the question I've been dying to ask for years.

But I can't. Not yet. "Maybe you should try again."

Eric pushes the sunglasses back to his eyes and switches his ball cap around so it's facing forward. After a few moments, he gives a tight nod. "Maybe I should."

He coughs, then—serious conversation apparently over—leans forward and points out the gorillas in their enclosure below. From up here, they appear small, almost cute. But I know that up close, they can be fierce, protective if they feel their loved ones are threatened.

Even though Eric is back to his witty, charming, joking self—retelling me the story of our tenth-grade field trip to the zoo when we got stuck on this very ride with the oh-so-full-of-himself football star Channing DePri, who kept making annoying monkey noises over the side of the tram car—I can't fully focus. I'm still thinking, still reeling over Eric's revelation.

That he used to like me. That we liked each other at the same time.

And I can't help wondering ... have those feelings faded for him? Or could he possibly ...? I can't even consider it, not until I know whether we could ever actually be together.

Just like he always does, he must sense something is off with me, because once we disembark from the ride near the Northern Frontier, he pulls at my elbow and puts his hands on both of my shoulders. "You doing okay? I know that some years, it's harder to do this than others."

He thinks I'm being quiet because I'm thinking of my mom. It isn't a shot in the dark. Every July 16, when I *should* be bringing her a gift and taking her out to lunch for her birthday—and instead, find myself here, alone with Eric, fighting tourists for a peek at the baby animals—I end up a tiny bit morose. It's good for me, to have this tradition, a way to remember fun times we had together, but it's also hard.

Life doesn't always turn out the way you want it to. It's chock full of those good-hard moments. And this man in front of me—my best friend, through thick and thin—knows it too.

I smile up at him, place my hands on top of his. If I can't speak the full truth to him, at least I can tell him this with absolute certainty. "There's nowhere I'd rather be right now. And no one I'd rather be with."

We stand there in the middle of the pathway for a long moment despite the ever-thickening crowd milling around us. Finally, Eric drops his hands, bops me on the nose, and says, "Race you to the polar bears."

And then he takes off—like always, bringing equal parts laughter and yearning to my life.

nine

. . .

IN A DIGITAL AGE of online donations, Venmo, and the like, you don't see old-fashioned carwash fundraisers as much anymore.

But Sonia insisted on building character in each of her young actors, said that her students wouldn't mooch off the goodwill of others without putting a little "pedal to the medal." One *could* argue that spending six out of seven days a week rehearsing for the show would be a lot of hard work, but apparently she wants to make us all sweat for it too.

Which is how I find myself on a Sunday afternoon surrounded by kids in the parking lot of Java Awakening—the coffee shop that Kayla's husband Josh manages—with a hose in my hand and a line of cars waiting to be washed. I'm on spraying duty, while each of the kids at the SUV I'm working on has a soapy sponge they're moving across the sleek black surface.

The sun is out and I've got on flip-flops, cutoff

shorts, and a pink T-shirt over my bathing suit. My hair is pulled into two low pigtails—not all of it can be pinned back, but I do what I can—and sunglasses have covered my eyes for the last two hours of work. Eric was on spraying duty before me, and I've still got wrinkled fingertips from all the times I dunked a sponge into a bucket of suds.

But despite all my terrible memories of feeling like a workhorse at past fundraisers as a teen—when the girls wore their bikini tops and golden skin while I rocked a one-piece and my sunburn just waiting to happen—it's different being the adult.

Kind of fun to squat down and show the littler kids how to clean a hubcap, and watch them run their hands across the top of the tire and come away filthy. Fun to tease the oldest middle school boys about cleaning the car roofs because they're so much taller than me.

Fun to let go of my worries for the day and just enjoy the moment.

"Hey, Miss P!" Linda, a confident sixth-grader, dips her sponge into the bucket at her feet, squeezes, lets the water fall back inside. "It's your song."

Did I mention that Sonia brought an old-school boom box and for the last half hour has been playing the *Cinderella* soundtrack? Yep, she really did. Which means everyone who is waiting for their car to be washed is also getting a show.

Kids are wiggling their booties, doing dance moves as they clean, waxing on and waxing off while belting the lyrics at the top of their lungs.

So far, I've held back. Just observed. But now, I'm not sure I can avoid it.

I'll try, though. It's one thing to sing on stage when I'm all warmed up and mentally prepared to do my best. But this?

Before I know it, Eric is beside me. He grabs the hose and sings into it quite loudly.

And terribly. It's like drunk karaoke on steroids. But there is no alcohol—only copious amounts of coffee and tea that's been fueling us for the last few hours. In fact, Prince Rob is inside getting us more right now.

At Eric's performance, the kids start yelling and covering their ears in laughing protest. I don't blame them—his voice truly is quite awful. And yet, he persists in singing like he's Idina Menzel letting go. When he sees I'm not singing along, he puts the "mic" next to my mouth and starts chanting "Miss P, Miss P, Miss P."

I fake glare at him but he grabs my hand and twirls me, shaking loose my laughter again. Meanwhile the music booms and practically all car washing has ceased. Oh, for heaven's sake. Fine. They want a show?

"Only if you all sing with me," I say.

Linda pumps her fist in the air and goes up on her toes into a spin of her own. Before I know it, I'm singing and the whole group is joining along, from the smallest six-year-old to the gangliest eighth-grader.

And … it's wonderful. Beautiful.

Fun.

For the first time since my song broke free in the

shower, I'm singing for the joy of it. And this time, I'm not alone.

I lift the hose into the air and shoot a zigzagging spray in triumph—a move that the patrons getting their cars washed do not seem to appreciate, judging by the frowns. But I can't even find it in myself to grimace or apologize, because now I'm holding out the fake mic to each kid as I circle the SUV and they sing into it, many of them dissolving into giggles.

We are crazy, and I love it.

When the song ends and another more low-key melody begins—and I spray off the soapy suds from the black vehicle—I find my way back to Eric, who is grinning and very pleased with himself.

"What?"

"Nothing," he says. "Just sounded good is all."

The kids bust out the towels and go to town. The car in front of ours is finished by another group and a new vehicle takes its place. I run over and wet down the surface of the sparkling blue Mustang before heading back to Eric. "You're lucky I'm not mad at you for that little stunt."

"Why would you be mad?" He turns to the kids at our car, who have just finished up the vehicle. There appears to be a break in the cars for now, although experience has shown we can get a new one at any moment. "Guys, she sounded amazing, right?"

"Well, yeah, Mr. M, but I agree with her." Twelve-year-old Tiffany snaps her gum and flips her long brown hair. "Not cool to put her on the spot like that."

"Totally not cool," her bestie, Liz, says.

All of my kids nod and echo the girls.

I fold my arms over my chest—not easy to do when holding a hose—and purse my lips. "See? Told you." And then, an idea hits. My lips curve up and I turn to my students. "Are you guys thinking what I'm thinking?"

Every single eye watching me lights up and everyone nods. They rush the buckets and dip their sponges—and step toward Eric.

"Shelbs." The warning in Eric's tone is edged with amusement. "You wouldn't. You're too nice."

I lift my hose and smile. "I grew up in a houseful of brothers. I had to learn to retaliate."

"But you never actually did." Eric steps forward, hands outstretched and reaching for the hose, as if it's a gun and he's trying to talk me down.

But it's too late, because I'm not the only one with a weapon.

"Charge!" Tiffany—I think—shouts.

I release a blast of water at Eric's chest while the kids rush him with sponges. He's covering his head and laughing, growling like a bear at the little ones, pretending to attack them—but the man is soaked and a soapy mess, pure and simple.

More kids join in the fun, abandoning the vehicle they're washing to attack Eric. And despite the fact Sonia is walking over, a stern look on her face, all I can do is giggle. Eventually I gather my wits and clap my hands. "All right, all right. Let's get back to work, friends. And let Mr. Moody breathe."

With some good-natured grumbling, the kids pull

away from him and he turns his full attention on me. Uh oh. I turn to run, but he's there before I know it, pulling me into a hug—and soaking my shirt in the process. "Eric!" I squeal as he rubs his soaped-up face into the crook of my neck, his stubble scratching the sensitive skin there.

Trying to wiggle away, I realize he's got me deadlocked so I place both of my hands on his chest and push. When that doesn't work—and after a few seconds of trying and failing to stop admiring the hard planes beneath my palms—I play dirty and tickle his sides.

But still he doesn't budge.

"Okay, Eric, you've gotten your revenge—which was not all that deserved since I was simply getting *you* back."

He pulls away, grinning. "You deserve all this and more, Shelby Phillips." Then he leans down, snatches up a wet sponge, and wrings it down the back of my neck.

I jump and stumble backward—right into Rob, who grabs for me before I can fall. When I yank open my eyes that I didn't know I'd closed, I find Rob's arms clutching my waist, keeping me upright.

And there's a carrier filled with Java Awakening drinks at our feet. Two of the drinks have fallen out, the brown liquid spilled across the asphalt.

"Oh, I'm so sorry."

His gaze flicks from my face back toward where Eric must still be standing, then back to me. He helps me straighten. "No problem. I can go get refills. You okay?"

"Oh, yeah. Great. We, um, just had a little water fight going out here."

"I can see that I missed the fun." He squats down and picks up what looks to be a passion tea drink that miraculously still has the lid on. When he stands, he holds it out to me. "I didn't know what you'd like, but thought this tea looked good." He scratches behind his ear and chuckles, low and throaty. "Thought it was pretty. Like you."

Oh. "Um, thank you." I take it from him and sip the tea. It's got a slight hint of fruit but nothing overpowering. And I'm guessing it's herbal, lacking the caffeine that my body is craving right now—because after that adrenaline rush, I'm gonna crash here pretty soon.

Rob just keeps staring at me, which is no surprise, because I'm sure I look awful.

I tuck a strand of hair that's come loose from my rubber band back behind my ear. "So—"

"Hey," he says at the same time. "I was thinking …"

"That's a dangerous habit," I tease.

He chuckles and rubs the back of his neck. "It definitely can be."

"What were you thinking?"

"I was wondering if you'd like to go out to dinner with me sometime this week? Maybe Tuesday night?"

I nearly choke on the liquid coming up from my straw. Whoa. I never expected this from him. I mean, sure, we've developed a camaraderie over the last few weeks. He's helped me a few more times with my singing, and me with his dancing. And I can't deny that he's handsome.

He's no Eric, and he can be a little awkward—though in a cute way—but he's not a creeper like Eric thought either. In fact, if there was no Eric in the picture, I might even like Rob as more than a coworker and friend.

Problem is, Eric *is* in the picture. And sure, I still don't know where we stand—after I brought it up yesterday, he hasn't said anything else about reactivating his ancestry account—but there's that tiny bit of hope. The fact that, since now I've told my friends how I feel about Eric, I've found it harder to keep from saying it to him.

So there's no room for Rob in my life, or even entertaining the idea of him.

Which is why I'm not sure how "That sounds nice" comes out of my mouth.

"Yeah? Great." His eyes dart behind me. "I'll text you with some dinner ideas. For now, Sonia is on the warpath. Beware."

Then he scoops up the trash at our feet and leaves me standing there with my drink and a hollowness in my stomach.

"What was that all about?" Eric eyes my cup. "And what are you drinking?"

"Rob got me a passion iced tea."

"You hate tea."

"I don't hate it."

"It's just not your favorite, right?" He rolls his eyes. "You're a coffee girl through and through. It's okay to say so."

That may be true, but ... "Why do I have to be pigeonholed? I can try new things." To prove it, I take another rather bland sip. It does nothing for me, but it really isn't terrible like I imagined it to be.

"Why would you want to try new things when you already know what you like?" And there's a hint of smugness, of superiority in his tone that rubs me a little bit the wrong way. Especially when he takes a step toward me, almost in challenge.

"Weren't you just telling me that change can be a good thing?" I take another step toward him and stand on my tiptoes. I'll never be taller than him, but he doesn't have the right to tower over me.

"Some change. But don't change yourself—who you are—for a guy, Shelbs."

What?! "I'm not."

"Okay." He says it sarcastically, like he doesn't believe me.

"It's just tea." I'm so confused. "When have I ever changed who I was for a guy?"

"I'm not saying you have. Just saying you shouldn't."

"Noted," I grumble. "We need to get back to the kids now." The cool breeze plus my wet shirt is starting to make me shiver a bit.

"I'm just saying, you don't have to let others push you around. If you want coffee instead of tea, ask for coffee." He tugs the tea out of my hand. "And if a guy asks you out and you don't want to go, say no."

Then, before I can say anything about it being rude to eavesdrop, Eric turns and walks toward the coffee shop entrance. He tosses my tea into a trash can and slams a palm against the door, opening it with a dramatic swing.

And once again, I'm left with my jaw on the ground, wondering what in the world just happened.

I normally sleep really well.

But ever since Eric became a guest in our house, sleep has been harder to come by. Add to that the sorta-kinda fight we had earlier today—well, given the fact it's now two a.m., I guess it was technically yesterday—and I've been lying here in bed staring at my ceiling for the last several hours, totally sleep deprived.

The scene has played out over and over in my mind. Several of the preteens approached me after the carwash, teasing me about how cute Eric and I were together. Even Sonia—Sonia!—told me she thought we made an adorable couple. When I told her we weren't together, she said, *"Why not, honey? If I was twenty years younger, I'd be giving you some competition."*

But it's Eric's expression—and his accusation about changing for a guy and doing something I don't want to do—that are giving me the most heartburn. Literally. (Never eat an entire half of a pizza in an attempt to drown your sorrows. It always comes back to haunt you. Or burn you, as it were. Ask me how I know this.)

He acted nonchalantly, but I can still see the stiffening of his shoulders, the angry bend of his lips, the strong tilt of his chin. And when he returned from inside Java Awakening, my favorite coffee in hand, I thanked him and set it on the curb—and didn't touch it again.

Eric and I don't fight often. In fact, I really can't remember the last time I was actually angry at him. Hurt, sure. But what has him so twisted up? If he likes me (as my friends seem to think), then why doesn't he just tell me so? And if he doesn't, he has no right to be upset if I want to date another guy.

But maybe I'm actually upset at the situation, not him. At the fact that I want him to want me—and yet, I can't want that.

My head hurts. Maybe an ice pack will offer some relief.

I climb out of bed and head down the hall, pausing before stepping into the living room. It's darkened except for the blue glow of the television set. My eyes take a few seconds to adjust and I realize Eric is sitting on the couch staring at the muted TV.

He punches the remote. "Hey."

"Hey."

Several long moments pass before I clear my throat and point toward the kitchen. "I was just going to get an ice pack."

"Headache?"

"Yeah." Then I start to move.

"Shelbs."

I pause next to Eric, look down at him—really look. Sitting on the couch with his feet propped on the coffee table, his hair is disheveled and his scruff is strong tonight, and he's wearing a white undershirt and blue and black checked pajama pants. He's so … casual. And at home.

Here. In *my* house.

My fingers dig into my palms as I clench fists on either side of my body.

He catches sight of them and grimaces. "I'm really sorry. I shouldn't have said what I did today. I was a total jerk."

Thank goodness he took my tension for anger instead of longing. But I don't want him to think I'm angry, don't want to fight. I hate not feeling at peace with my friends, especially Eric. So I step over his legs and slide onto the cushion beside him. "You *were* kind of a jerk," I say softly.

"Ugh, I know." Slinking down a bit, he lays his head on the cushion behind him. "Can you forgive me?"

"Of course." I pause. "But why did you say those things? Do you really think I would change who I am for a guy?"

"No. I don't. You're too smart for that. Although …"

"Although what?"

The refrigerator's hum in the kitchen behind us fills in the silence.

"Never mind. It's not any of my business."

"Considering you're my best friend, of course it is." I shift so I'm sitting sideways, my feet tucked under me, my head propped up on my hand as I look at him. "I want to know your opinion about everything."

"Even your love life?"

Oh boy. My fingers tingle and I swallow hard. "Even that."

"Okay." Eric's nose scrunches as he studies me, his eyes following the contours of my face. "Do you *want* to go on a date with Rob? I mean, if you really like him, that's great. But I kind of got the impression that you felt pressured into going out with him."

I take it back. I do *not* want to talk with him of all people about this. Especially because I really can't get a read on him—on why he even cares.

And I'm terrified to ask.

But I have to.

I tuck my bottom lip under my teeth for a few seconds and consider what to say—how to stay on this tightrope between us without rushing forward, without falling off. "I don't *not* like him. We have a lot in common. I admit, I was surprised at him asking me out—"

"I wasn't." He grunted. "Remember? I told you he liked you from the beginning."

"True. But I didn't think someone like him would be interested in me."

"What does *that* mean? You're incredible." He shuts his eyes briefly, shakes his head. "I'm honestly surprised you haven't dated more guys like Rob. More guys, period."

"I've dated." No, I'm not like Eric, the effervescent funny man that women have fawned over since middle school—and I've had to watch him date countless of them. Although, to be fair, he hasn't really dated at all for the last year or so.

"*You've* dated?" He spears me with a look that says he knows better. "When?"

"What about Trevor?" My fifteen-year-old self thought the clarinet player was cute and smart, though my twenty-six-year-old self can see he never stood a chance. Not when compared with Eric. But at that point, I hadn't yet admitted to myself that I was in love with my best friend.

"Trevor? Seriously? We alllll knew *that* wasn't going anywhere. That dude was super annoying."

"What was so annoying about him?"

"I don't know. He was just … always there."

I poke him in the ribs. "It hardly qualifies as annoying to have a boyfriend who likes hanging out with you."

He snatches my finger and holds it firm, not letting go. "Fine, it was annoying for me." Then he frowns and lowers our hands to the couch, where he takes more of my hand than just my finger in his. "That's why I was a jerk today. Because I realized that eventually you're going to date, get married—and I'm going to lose you."

Whoa. "No, you won't."

"Shelby, I will. It's only natural. No guy will want another dude hanging around all the time. Believe me. If you were my wife …" He shakes his head, looks up at the ceiling before huffing out a strained laugh. "Anyway, you've been part of my life since forever, and I hate the idea of anything changing."

Anything?

His eyes dart back to me and oh no, I must have said that question out loud. I swear he must be able to hear my heart beating like a drumline in my chest, but he doesn't say anything—just keeps watching me. We stare at each other, and I want so badly to abandon all doubts, to give in to the irresistible pull of Eric's blue eyes in the semi-darkness.

Instead, I veer back to the topic at hand. I *want* to tell him about the genetic testing, but it just doesn't feel like the right timing. "Maybe the reason I haven't dated much is that I haven't found someone worth spending my time on." *AKA, someone better than you.* "What's your excuse?" Then, maybe it's the darkness or the fact I'm exhausted, but I flirt on the edge of danger just a little bit. "Why haven't *you* dated much in recent years?"

My fingers are still entwined with his and I feel the faintest brushing of his thumb over my knuckles—or I imagine I do, anyway. I don't dare look down, away from his gaze.

Eric shrugs. "I needed to figure some stuff out about my own life before bringing someone else into it."

"Needed to? As in past tense?"

"Maybe. I don't know." He sits up, shifts so he's sideways now too, facing me more fully. A bit more closely too. "There's still more to figure out, but I'm finally at the point where I'm ready to be serious with someone."

I can't breathe. Just … can't.

Because I swear, it's like he's saying he wants me to be that someone. But he's not saying it too.

Oh my word, I honestly have no idea *what* he's saying.

"Speaking of figuring things out"—he continues—"I

reactivated my profile on the ancestry site yesterday after our conversation. And I got a match."

"What?" I straighten in my seat. "Are you serious? Why didn't you lead with that?"

"Guess I'm still processing how I feel about it. I think … I think I'm excited. But also kinda freaked, you know?"

I grip his hand tighter. "Of course. That's natural, I'd think. So who is it? Does it tell you your relationship?"

"An uncle on my bio mom's side. He actually lives in Monterey. Can you believe it? I have a relative just eight hours away."

"It's incredible." I fling myself at him and pull him into a hug. "I'm so happy for you."

And me. I mean, that's completely selfish, I know, but … but what if this could be the answer to my prayers? What if Eric could have a relationship with his uncle? And what if that led to cousins, aunts … maybe even siblings? First of all, incredible for him. After so many years of feeling alone.

Second of all, incredible for us—*if* he feels the same way about me.

"So what are you going to do?" I pull back to look at him, but he tugs me to his chest again. You won't hear me complaining.

"I wrote to him. Asked if … if maybe I could visit. Haven't heard back yet. But if I do, would you come with me?"

Eric never asks for much, so the fact he is vulnerable enough to ask this of me means something. "Of course."

"Thanks, Shelby. You're a good friend."

Oh, how I despise that word, especially in this moment. But maybe we are on the cusp of erasing it—or rather, enhancing it.

I can't help but wonder what he's thinking when he settles against the couch and pats his knee. "Lay down. I'll rub your head."

When I look at him funny, his lips curl upward. "I thought you had a headache."

Oh. "Right." So I scootch down a tad and stretch out on the couch, my head on his lap.

His fingers gently find my hair and massage my temples. The couch is soft beneath me and I'm floating on a bed of clouds. I can't help the yawn that exits my mouth. The TV screen flickers back to life, but quickly switches from a sports station to *The Sound of Music*.

I reach up and squeeze his knee in thanks, and I fall asleep dreaming of my own favorite things—one in particular.

ten

. . .

I DIDN'T THINK I'd have to kiss him.

Rob, that is.

This is a children's show, for goodness sake. Why do the prince and Cinderella need to kiss onstage? Can't we just hug? Fist bump? Or, at the very least, fake it? That's what we've done every other time we've rehearsed this scene.

But no. Sonia has just informed us that there will be lip-on-lip action. My mouth has just dropped. Half the kids are yelling "Ewww" at the top of their lungs. The other half are making obnoxious kissing noises.

As for Rob? He waggles his eyebrows at me and smiles—and I've honestly never had the urge to hit someone like I want to hit him.

Because I didn't think it could get worse than having to dance and sing and SPEAK in front of other people.

But I was wrong. Sooooo wrong. And here he is

acting like it's no big deal. Maybe to him, it's not. Probably he has a ton more kissing experience than I do. Though truth be told, the middle school girls here probably have more kissing experience than I do. I've only had one boyfriend ever, remember? And that was over a decade ago! I am woefully out of practice.

And everyone is about to know it.

I feel like making an announcement: *Excuse me. Whoever is in charge of the stage's trap door, now would be a great time to pull it. Please and thank you.*

Sure that my face is flaming brighter than a star billions of miles away, I blink down at Sonia, who is in front of the stage where Rob and I are standing. "Do you think maybe—"

"Shelby, you're going to be fine. Rob's a nice guy." Sonia gestures to him. "Right, Rob?"

"I try." He chuckles then elbow bumps me.

But I'm not in an elbow-bumping mood. In fact, I can barely move. I'm rooted to the stage with icicles for feet. "It's not that."

"Honestly, in all my years of directing, and acting before that, I've realized that the easiest way to get over the awkwardness of an onstage kiss is to just try it. Then you can talk through the technical parts later." Our director waves her hand in the air. "Of course, do what you're comfortable with, but I believe this is going to be a powerful moment, and don't want it cheapened with a fake kiss."

I want to scream that the audience won't know it's fake, but again—hi, I'm still Elsa over here. And now, my ears are buzzing.

Maybe I'm not meant to do this after all. This kind of thing wouldn't bother a real performer, would it? Mom did countless shows in her younger years, and she used to tell me about them all. She laughed at the kissing—even bragged about locking lips with a guy from her favorite sitcom once upon a time in a high school play, before he was famous.

Oh, how I wish she was here in this moment, to offer advice. To help me laugh at myself. Wait, Eric's good at that. Where is he? I need him right now.

Biting my lip, my gaze travels throughout the auditorium, which is filled with all the kids. Many are on their phones so aren't paying attention. Others' eyes bore into me. But Eric is nowhere to be found, which probably means he's out putting the finishing touches on the set.

"Sounds good," Rob says, shaking me from my thoughts. Then he turns to me. "You okay with this?"

It's actually kind of him to ask and makes me feel a tiny bit better. At least I don't have to kiss a complete stranger or a guy with missing teeth and greasy hair. Gotta take the wins where I can. "A little nervous," I manage. "But yeah, it's okay."

He leans in a bit. "I'm nervous too." At the raise of my brow, he nods. "Seriously. You make me nervous, Shelby."

Oh. Right. Because he likes me. Because we're still supposed to go on a date tomorrow night even though the only guy I can really think about is Eric—and the fact that there's a chance for us.

Which means I should really tell Rob that I can't go

out with him. It's not fair to date one person while loving another. But I can't say that right now, because that would make this moment even more awkward.

I'll tell him later. For sure.

Right after I kiss him.

Oh my goodness, kill me now.

I clear my throat. "Um, so, what should we do first?"

"Well." He tilts his head, and the lights from overhead are reflected in his eyes. "I could put my hand here"—on the waist—"and you could throw yours around my neck?"

I comply, and now we look like a couple of high schoolers at a freshman dance.

He tugs on my waist gently, moving me closer to him. "Then, I guess I could just … I don't know. Kiss you?"

I snort. "That easy, huh?"

"Basically." His smile should put me at ease, but the word makes me stiffen instead. Because there's nothing basic about it.

Especially not when, out of the corner of my eye, I finally see Eric leaning against the wall. His expression is completely neutral, but he's got his arms crossed over his chest. It's like the dance lessons all over again, except this time I don't think he'll be pulling me aside to demonstrate.

The very idea brings a flush to my whole body.

I redirect my gaze to Rob, looking up, up, up into his eyes before nibbling my bottom lip. "So, um, does my nose go right or left?"

"Let's say left."

"Right." Okay.

"Right?"

"Oh, no. I mean left."

His eyes crinkle at the corners. "Left it is, then."

I open my mouth to agree. Before a word comes out, Rob tugs me close and tries to kiss my lips. But as I said, my mouth is open.

So he kisses my teeth instead.

I jerk back, a hand over my lips. "Sorry! I didn't know we were going yet."

"My bad. I thought it would be easier to just get it over with instead of worrying about the details."

And that's when I hear the laughter peeling through the theater. See the kids' faces screwed up, see them pointing at me. Whispers bend and coil through the air before smacking me in the face. Even Sonia's face registers amusement.

And it's like I'm back there—the day of my audition, when I was the butt of all the jokes.

When everyone knew I had no business being on stage. Not anymore.

What am I doing here? What am I playing at? I thought I was growing in this area. I should be beyond this embarrassment, but I'm not. And I hate that. It's only further proof that this whole thing was a terrible idea.

But no matter how terrible an idea, I made a commitment. So I stay instead of run.

Thank goodness Sonia takes mercy on me and

declares rehearsal over for today. Amongst the children's cheers, Rob squeezes my hand. "Don't worry. We'll get it right."

"I know," I manage with a weak smile.

As kids exit out the back of the auditorium, Sonia approaches the stage. "Great work, you two. Just keep communicating and practicing that moment and you'll be right as rain."

Keep practicing. Oy vey.

Rob sticks his hands in his pockets. "You want to stay after and practice some more?"

"No!" And oops, I did NOT mean to yell that. "I mean, sorry. I have … plans." Sudden plans to curl up in a ball on our couch and binge-watch Gene Kelly musicals, but Rob does *not* need to know that. "Maybe we can practice more tomorrow?"

He gapes for a beat, then recovers and nods, and there's still a bit of uncertainty in it. "Wherever the night leads, right?"

And then I realize what I said. Because I meant tomorrow as in right after rehearsal. But maybe he thought I meant tomorrow, as in our date.

I'm about to drop to my knees and pry open the wished-for trap door myself.

Thankfully, Rob gives me a quick hug and takes off upstage toward the door that leads to the hallway. Maybe he's going to his classroom to rehearse some more or prep for the upcoming school year? I probably could use the extra vocal practice, but right now, I don't want to be anywhere near here.

I grab my things from backstage and head for the

parking lot, but end up walking toward the playground instead. Where there used to be sand, now wood chips fill in the space underneath the blue play structure, the swing set, the large climbing dome. A few ramadas boast picnic tables and offer shade from the sun, which hasn't seemed to make up its mind about coming out to play today.

I would have expected to see a few stragglers out here waiting for their parents, but the whole campus seems deserted. Hard to believe that in a little over a month, it will fill with life. I'll get a new classroom with adorable five and six-year-olds, a chance to infuse knowledge and love into them. I'll come home exhausted but satisfied every day from a job I love. I'll help out with future theater shows from the sidelines.

Those things are a given.

But it's the rest—the uncertainty of where Eric and I stand, of whether his uncle will ever reply to his email, whether I'm fooling myself in hoping that we will ever be anything more than friends—that's got my insides truly twisted.

Not even my worry over the show can rival all of *that*.

I walk through the wood chips, my feet a bit unsteady, and find myself below the bubble where Eric found me all those years ago. It's in even rougher shape now, discolored by its days in the sun. If I could, I'd climb inside and disappear again. How silly is that? Because I'm an adult, and adults do not climb inside plastic playground tubes as a way of dealing with their problems.

It is sad how much my instincts are telling me otherwise, though.

My whole body hums with nostalgia and I pull myself through the thin ropes of the clatter bridge, which is made of brown slats that move when someone walks over them. I lie down and gaze up at the fluffy white clouds in the sky. It's surprisingly peaceful.

I stay like that for a while until I hear footsteps approaching.

"There you are." Eric's face appears above me.

"Hey." I push up to a sitting position, duck under the rope, and let my legs dangle off the edge of the bridge.

He stays standing in front of me. "So, that was kind of rough in there, huh?"

"You could say that again."

"So, that was—"

"Eric." I smirk, but then I'm somber again, wincing with one eye open. "How bad was it?"

"The kiss?"

"Mmm hmm."

"Very toothy."

I kick at him, but he steps out of range. "Yeah, well, it took me off guard. Although ..." Shrugging, I look away.

Without seeing, I can sense him move close again. "Although what?" The citrus in his cologne tickles my nose, putting all of my senses on high alert. What's happening to me? I used to be so good at ignoring these little triggers, but lately it's like I give myself an inch, and my body takes a freaking twenty thousand leagues.

Finally, I meet his gaze again. "It's not like the kiss was destined to be great."

"I know. You had to kiss *Rob*." He says his name like there's a mothball in his mouth.

I laugh quietly. "No, it's me. I'm the problem." Ugh, do I admit this to him? But whatever else might be between us, he's my best friend first and foremost. I can tell him anything. Well, almost anything. "I haven't kissed anyone in eleven years."

"Don't tell me. Trevor?"

At my pathetic nod, he rubs a hand down his face and groans. "No! Oh, Shelbs, you've been robbed. That dude was pimply and a metal mouth to boot."

"True, his braces were not the most fun. Especially that one time my earring got caught on them. Don't ask."

Eric guffaws.

A breeze trips across my cheeks, cooling and soothing them. "But other than today's disaster of a kiss with Rob, *that dude* is the only experience I've got. And I know it shouldn't be a big deal, but it's just ... like, I don't know. It's stupid." My chest tightens as the anxiety creeps back into my heart. I gulp in a big breath.

"Hey." Eric's voice softens. "Nothing about you is stupid."

"This should come more naturally for me."

"Kissing?"

I kick at him again, this time connecting with his outer thigh. But it's more like a tap than a kick. "Hardy har. No, performing. Kissing onstage is part of performing, just like singing and dancing. But no matter how much I practice, how much I picture performing on opening night, there's part of me that still feels paralyzed. I still feel like I'm not living up to Mom's legacy."

A dumb tear falls and before I can push it away, Eric's thumb swipes at it.

I continue. "The last thing she said to me was to be brave. Then, after she … well, Dad told us we each had to carry on her legacy. And I've tried. But I'm just not as brave as she was."

On stage … or off. Sure, I've had moments of bravery, of hope that I can live up to her legacy, but I still am stuck in this place of indecision when it comes to Eric. I feel my walls crumbling, my weaknesses becoming more apparent, and I don't know how to be strong. I don't know what's right or wrong anymore.

And then Eric's there, close, hand on my cheek, staring into my eyes. "Shelbs." His breath is minty and soft, warm. "Your mom's legacy isn't her singing. It's your family. It's you. And I'd bet my favorite Padres hat that your mom would be so proud of who you are."

"You're that confident, huh?" No one comes between Eric and his Padres hat. Once when we were kids, Cody stole and tried to hide it and … yeah, not pretty.

Eric crosses his heart. "I didn't have countless years with her, but anyone who spent even an hour around your mom knows that kindness marked everything she did. And you … you're just like that. You're a survivor, Shelbs. You're *so* brave. Which means you're just like her in all the ways that matter."

Somehow, without my knowledge, my hand has drifted from my lap to his chest, and my fingers grip at his shirt. "You really think so?" Because that's all I've ever wanted to be. Kind and selfless, brave like Mom who—on her deathbed—was more concerned with how *I* was doing than the fact she was wracked with pain.

"I do." Eric leans in, presses his forehead against mine.

We stay like that for several long moments, and I'm comfortable, safe—but scorched too. I have to change the subject, and pronto. Pulling back, I force a chuckle. "Being kind and brave is great, but it won't help me kiss better."

Eric gets a strange look on his face, and he presses his lips together. "Remember how I told you a few weeks ago that I'd do whatever I could to help you with the show?"

"Yeah. And running lines with me has been a godsend. Pretty sure Alexis would rather watch a chick flick than help me with that."

"Probably." Opening his mouth to say something, he snaps it shut just as quickly.

A wriggle of uncertainty crawls through me. "What is it?"

"I just had a thought, but ..." He shakes his head. "I don't know. It might be ..."

"Might be ...?" I coax.

"I'd never want to make you uncomfortable." Eric kicks at the wood chips below. "But I could, you know, help you practice."

My nose scrunches. "You've *already* helped me practice."

"Not with your lines. With your ... kissing."

Oh. Ooooohhhhhh.

Hi there. I'm Shelby Elise Phillips and if you're reading this, it means I'm dead.

Because I am. Dead, that is. What in the world is happening? Am I in some alternate, wonderful universe where my sexy best friend of seventeen years just offered to PRACTICE KISS ME?

My silence is long—because, remember, I'm dead—and Eric must take it as a sign that I am horrified by the idea. His cheeks color and he shakes out a laugh. "Yeah, I'm a total weirdo for suggesting—"

"Okay!" Praise, Jesus, folks, I'm alive once more. Although my blunt resurrection and overenthusiasm might themselves be cause for dying of embarrassment again.

"Okay?" He licks his lips.

"Sure. I mean, yeah, if you think you could help." *Don't make it weird, Shelby.* This is just one best friend helping out another. Not that I could see Lauren or Alexis doing this for me. Not that I would want them to. But still.

"I just thought, you know, the more practice you get, the more confident you'll feel for the stage. With Rob."

"Right. Yes." My head bobs in quick succession, eager to show Eric that I'm totally cool with this. That it totally makes sense.

When in reality, I know I'm playing a dangerous game here. It's Russian roulette and my heart stands to come out with a bullet-sized hole.

"All right, then." Eric grabs onto the rope on either

side of me. Our faces are level with one another and oh so close. "So, where to start?"

I have to laugh or I'll combust with his nearness. "You're the kissing expert, not me."

"I'm an expert now, am I?" His teasing grin shoots straight through me, up and into all my limbs, which radiate fire and ice. "Well, as a famous movie once said, 'you gotta pucker up your lips, like dis.'" He proceeds to do so in the most dramatic fashion, apparently imitating Sebastian the crab from *The Little Mermaid*.

"Oh wow, I was definitely doing it wrong. So like this?" I push my lips outward and bat my eyes for good effect.

"Perfect. You're totally ready to kiss and be kissed now."

And yet, despite his words, he just stands there, looking at me. Is he waiting for me to do something? He's supposed to be the teacher. But maybe he does need a little encouragement, so I give his shirt a gentle tug.

That seems to be all he needs—because then my best friend swoops in and kisses me without further ado. It's quick and soft and sweet and over far too soon, before I can even enjoy the moment. This thing I've dreamed about for years … done.

He exhales heavily and studies me. "Well?"

"Um." I nibble at my bottom lip. He zeroes in on it, and his pupils darken. Oh, goodness. I know I shouldn't say what I'm about to—the tightrope is frayed, nearly ready to snap me loose into oblivion—but this is heady, being so near him. Feeling his lips graze mine.

And I want more.

"I think … we should keep practicing."

"If you insist." His mouth meets mine again, tentative at first—closed off but savoring. I loop my arms around his neck to steady myself against him, nudging my fingertips into the hair at the base of his neck. Meanwhile, one of his hands finds my back, the other pushing its way up into my hair.

My whole body trembles with the pleasure of this moment, of discovering a new side to this man I have known—and loved—for so long. His kiss deepens and my lips part to welcome him more fully. A deep sigh ekes from somewhere inside of me, and this only seems to make Eric's kisses come faster.

Is he as afraid as I am of this moment ending?

I pull back slightly, but Eric takes the opportunity to angle his head downward, drawing a line with his mouth from the corner of my lips along my jaw. His hand cups my head, his thumb stroking the outer shell of my ear as his gentle kisses press fire into every single pore they touch.

And when they reach the spot just below my earlobe, I suck in a tight gasp just before my breath shudders out again. But it's not just *my* breathing that's ragged. Eric's breaths come in spurts too.

Knowing that he's got me, I slide off the bridge and press up onto my toes so I can reach his mouth again with mine. My hands take his face between them—the stubble along his jaw is softer than it looks—and his are at my waist, fingertips skimming the skin just above my shorts. I stroke my thumbs along his cheekbones and deepen the kiss, as hungry in this moment for Eric as a teenage girl on an extreme diet.

And he seems to be just as ravenous.

Seconds, minutes, who knows how much time flies by, but finally my subconscious grows louder than the pleasure. *He's not yours yet. He's got dreams outside of you, and you owe him the truth before things go any further between you. Before this becomes real and there's no going back.* And I know my inner Jiminy Cricket is right. No matter what I am feeling, how my heart is singing, I cannot yet give in. I can't risk Eric's resentment in the future.

So I break our kiss. There's silence between us, and because I can't stand awkward silences, I say the first thing that comes to mind. "Sorry. That was weird, wasn't it?"

What? Shelby! What are you saying? It wasn't weird. It was wonderful. Too wonderful for words, really.

Eric blinks, shoves a hand through his hair. Chuckles. "Yeah. Super weird." He coughs. "Well, maybe stick with the first kind of kiss for Rob. On stage, at least. What you do during your date tomorrow night is your own business."

Why is he bringing *that* up? "I—"

"Hopefully that was helpful." Eric shrugs. "That's all it was meant to be."

Maybe he's reacting to my outburst, or maybe this really *was* nothing to him. But that can't be true. The way he kissed me … I swear it wasn't nothing. "Eric."

"It's getting late. I should go." He steps back and stuffs his hands into his pockets. "Got plans with the guys, so I'll probably get home super late. Don't wait up or anything."

Then he turns and trudges through the playground toward the parking lot, leaving me with an aching loss I haven't felt since my mother died.

eleven

. . .

THERE ARE few things worse than waking up with a gut full of regret. Not even a stomach virus can top it. At least with a physical illness, you can purge and feel immediately better.

But when you fear you've made the biggest mistake of your life and broken something that might just be unfixable? That sits and lingers until your stomach is so heavy you can't move.

That's why I called in to rehearsal sick today. Why I have avoided Eric at all costs, locking myself in my room since I got home last night, only emerging to grab some water and use the restroom—and only when I'm sure he's not home (after all, *he* went to rehearsal to finish up the sets).

It's also why I canceled the date with Rob tonight. Although, truth be told, I was planning to do that anyway. There's no way, with the state of my mind, that

I could give the guy a fair shot. Eric's rejection is all I can think about.

So, yeah. It's been a long, heavy day—and not even a musical-watching marathon on my laptop and a bag of Skittles has been able to bring me out of the doldrums. I'm sitting very stuck in the very bottom drum, way down deep.

My phone vibrates on the bed next to me. I consider ignoring it, but it might be Evie. They were supposed to find out the gender of their baby today, though Connor wanted to keep it a secret. (Doesn't he know Evie is terrible at keeping secrets? Girl has absolutely no poker face.)

Or maybe it's Lauren, giving an update on her travels. (Topher is taking her to Italy before she has to come home this weekend.)

Whoever it is, maybe they can provide me with a distraction from the fact I may have ruined the best relationship in my life. I reach for the phone, sit up against my headboard—and groan. The text is from Eric. And he's being completely sweet.

Eric: *You feeling any better? I could bring you some soup on my way home in about an hour.*

My thumb's pad caresses the smooth surface of the screen. Could I be making up the awkwardness between us? I mean, I haven't seen him since the fiasco yesterday, but this message seems to indicate that all is well.

Me: *Yeah, feeling a little better.*

That's true.

Me: *And I'm fine. Thank you, though.*

I pause. Do I end it there or engage further? Even

though Eric and I have never had trouble communicating, it seems less daunting via text for some reason. Maybe I can feel him out this way.

Me: *How are you? Did you get the sets all done?*

While I wait for the three little dots on the message to materialize into actual words, I glance at the clock on my white bedside table. Whoa. Already seven in the evening. I shouldn't be surprised, what with the sunlight waning through the curtains of my window. Soon it will disappear completely, and I've accomplished exactly nothing today.

Finally, my phone buzzes again in my hand.

Eric: *Mostly. Jon and Craig were screwing around and spilled a whole bucket of primer on the concrete so we wasted time cleaning that up.*

I chuckle, the tightness in my stomach already loosening a tad. Just as I'm about to respond, another message comes in.

Eric: *So.*

The dots hover again. Ugh. That "so" sounded (looked?) very ominous. When the next text appears, I pull it closer to my face, my heartbeat erratic.

Eric: *Heard back from my uncle. He can meet up on Saturday night for a late dinner. That would mean we'd have to leave rehearsal a bit early to drive up, and I know the show would be less than a week after that. So I understand if you can't come with me anymore.*

Oh no, he doesn't.

Me: *Trying to uninvite me from the biggest moment of your life? I don't think so.*

His reply doesn't come right away. Finally …

Eric: *I just didn't know if you'd be able to get away. Or if things were weird now.*

Guess I'm *not* the only one feeling the tension from across the miles and distance between us, which might as well be a canyon for as close as we've been, especially lately. But I will not let one ill-conceived kiss ruin seventeen years of friendship. I won't. Besides, he shouldn't have to pay for my hurt feelings over a rejection he probably didn't even know he was giving. It's clear I misread his feelings in this. But just because he doesn't feel the same way about me doesn't mean he should lose me as a friend.

So … I lie.

Me: *You mean because of the kiss? Things aren't weird. Like you said, you were just helping me out. That's all it was.*

Eric: *Okay. Glad we cleared that up.*

Me: *Me too.*

Eric: *So … Saturday? We'd have to spend the night in his town, but I found a hotel and booked us a few rooms.*

Me: *So sure I would say yes, were you?*

I smile at the thought. Yes, it will take more than this little kissing incident to break up the powerful duo of Shelby and Eric.

Eric: *I knew you couldn't say no to this charming face.*

Then he texts me a picture of him cross-eyed, sticking his tongue out and pushing his nose up with a fingertip to resemble a pig's snout. Shaking my head, I send my own photo of me giving him my best "unamused teacher face," as he likes to call it.

Eric: *Ooo, I've annoyed you. Guess I'd better get you that* *soup after all. See you soon. And Shelbs, thanks. I'm actually not sure I could go without you.*

My hand clutches the locket at my throat and I consider how to reply—whether to reply at all. So I settle for a heart emoji. A yellow one, not red. For friendship and all that.

Seconds later, my door bounces open and Alexis steps inside the room. She's wearing dark skinny jeans and a tight orange T-shirt that matches her hair with a yellow vest over the top. "I take it by the looks of you that you didn't go on your date."

"And I take it that you just got home from work after going in so early this morning that you were gone before I even woke up."

"Ooo, touché. Shelby Phillips, what has gotten into you, being all sassy back to me? It's a good look on you."

I sigh. "I didn't mean to be sassy, though I am concerned about you working so many hours stuck behind a computer."

"You should feel more sorry for me that I have to deal with the likes of Dax Nyhart." Alexis's face contorts and her tongue flicks out like she's tasted something rancid. "He landed the account I was working so hard for. That makes two promotions and ten accounts that he's gotten over me, and all within the last year since he started working for his uncle. And let me tell ya—he's not that good. My boss is just playing favorites because Dax is family. And it's infuriating."

"Aw, I'm sorry, friend." I pat the mattress next to me.

"Want to watch something with me to make yourself feel better?"

She eyes my computer open on the bed. "No offense, but I think I'd tear my hair out if I had to listen to that stuff you call music." Tugging on her long braid, she waggles her eyebrows. "And my hair is my best feature."

"I thought that was your sarcasm," I tease.

"Ha. That's true. You can put that on my gravestone someday." She eyes me up and down, pointing at my greasy half-ponytail on the top of my head. "Speaking of hair, what's with yours? Have you been in here all day or something? The air in this room feels stale."

Pivoting the lower half of my body, I dangle my feet over the edge of the bed and stretch. "I couldn't make myself go to rehearsal today."

"Did you choke again?"

Only Alexis would be that blunt. (Kayla's blunt too, but she's got a tiny bit of compassion and tact. Alexis … you've gotta dig for them.) But I laugh—and I guess that's a good thing. Because if I can laugh about it, my failures on stage haven't scarred me too badly. "Well, I did have to kiss Rob for the first time yesterday and his lips landed on my teeth, so there's that."

At Alexis's guffaw, I stand. "But the real reason I stayed in bed is what happened after rehearsal."

Her eyebrows rise. "That sounds like a good walking story. Wanna join me? You need to get out of this room and I need to burn some fury."

"All right. Give me a second to get dressed."

"I'll change into something more comfortable and

we can meet at the front door in five." Before I can agree, she heads toward the master bedroom at the end of the hallway and shuts the door.

"Sure, Alexis. I'd be glad to," I say to no one.

Laughing to myself, I make quick work of finding some clean shorts and a comfy tank and slipping on my tennis shoes. Then I meet Alexis and we lock up and head down the sidewalk. Our very attractive neighbor Ryan waves from his driveway, where he's washing his pickup truck while listening to country music. Alexis ignores him but I smile and wave back. "He's going to think you hate him."

"Why should I care what a man thinks about me?" She picks up her pace and the breeze blows back her hair from her stony face. "In my experience, the majority of men only want to use a woman for their own purposes. I'm much happier staying away from them altogether. Even if they do look hot while washing their vehicle."

Oh, friend. I want to reach out and hug her, but Alexis Matkin would never allow it. Still, I can't let this moment pass without acknowledging her pain—whatever it is. "You want to talk about it?"

"Nope. We're not talking about me tonight. Why didn't you go on your date with the fake prince? Was he a jerk about the kiss?"

The sidewalk dips and turns as we head down a hill. In the distance, the ocean spreads across the horizon like hot oil in a pan. "Nothing like that. Rob is really nice, actually. And from the time we've spent together outside of rehearsal, I've learned we have a lot in common. We love kids, musicals. He's easy to get along with, and he's got a great voice."

"But he's not Eric."

"No." I inhale a deep breath before diving into my story. "I also decided to cancel our date because I didn't feel well after I kissed Eric yesterday." The words tumble out so fast they're a jumbled mess.

Alexis pulls up short and grabs my elbow. "I'm sorry, what?"

The elderly couple getting into their vehicle in front of the house across the street glances our way. I wave to let them know that Alexis's shriek is nothing to be concerned about before redirecting my attention to my friend. "It wasn't a real kiss. At least, I don't think so."

Then I tell her everything about yesterday afternoon. About the texts today. And it feels good, like someone turned the pressure valve down a notch and I can breathe again.

When I'm done, we've walked a mile and Alexis is silent. The sun has exchanged places with the moon, which is full and nearly iridescent in the black sky.

"That doesn't sound like a practice kiss to me, Shelby. It sounds like years of pent-up passion finally brimming to the surface."

That's what I had thought too. Only … "Then why did he act like it was nothing?"

"To be fair, you did that first with your comment about it being weird."

"Ugh." As we descend a hill, my view of the sea diminishes. The water sparkles and winks at me as it disappears. "I wondered if that was it. So you think he might actually …?"

"Love you back?"

"Not love, necessarily. But like me?"

"Oh, he definitely likes you. And now that he's got a biological connection to someone else, what are you freaking waiting for? Wasn't that your only hang-up? Go on this trip with him and when the moment is right, you kiss that man again."

"You sound like Kayla." I try to tease, but my voice is tight.

"I can admit when I'm wrong—"

She cuts off at the look I give her.

"I can!" She frowns. "Maybe Kayla has a point. Kissing has a way of bringing true feelings to the surface. So this time, you kiss him, and tell him you mean it."

Despite the coolness in the air, the thought produces sweat on my palms. "I can't do that."

She stops walking and puts her hands on her hips. "Look, Shelby, I know it's out of character having me of all people encourage you like this. But Eric is one of the rare breed of men who's actually not of the swine variety, and you love him. It's time to be brave, girl. Be honest and true to yourself. I've seen you conquer so much this last month, with the musical and everything else. You can do this." And then, she shocks me by grabbing my hand and squeezing. "It's what your mom would want for you. To be happy."

And I know she's right. But I can't deny that I'm scared. Deathly afraid of losing everything. Still, if things worked out—if Eric was willing to leap into the unknown with me, even after I tell him that I can't have kids—then it would be worth the risk, wouldn't it?

Before I can pull Alexis into a hug, she lets go of me and holds up her hand. "Besides, you're super mopey lately, and I'm tired of it."

If I didn't know any better, I'd think Alexis meant it. But I see beyond the upturned tip of her nose and the defiant gaze to the ever so slight twinkle in her eye.

"Alexis, someday, a man is going to sweep you off your amazing feet and you're not going to know what to do with yourself."

"You take that blasphemy back right now. If any man ever tries to pick me up, he'll get whacked in the you-know-whats." Grinning (because apparently the thought of violence makes her happy?), she slings an arm around my shoulders. "Now, how about we head home and watch something like you suggested? I'm in the mood for a little *Die Hard* action. You down?"

Normally I'd just go along with her suggestion, what she wants, but tonight I'm feeling a little freer to speak my mind. "Actually, how about something a bit less … bloody?"

She frowns. "I refuse to watch some sappy rom-com. Not tonight, when I feel like throwing darts at a target with Dax's face on it. Ooo, I wonder if I could order one?"

"That seems a bit extreme." I laugh. "How about something in between? Isn't there at least one of those superhero movies with a bit of romance in it?"

As we walk, she purses her lips. "All right, fine. *Thor* it is. See? I can be reasonable."

And I can be honest about what I want without making people upset. Such a small thing, the selection of a movie, but it's a big lesson that I've struggled with all my life.

But will it translate to every other facet of my life—including my relationship with Eric?

twelve

. . .

WHY CAN'T anything ever go according to plan?

"What was that noise?" My hands fly to the seatbelt across my chest and I turn wide eyes to Eric, whose cheeks have gone pale.

We're five or six hours into our road trip—which, thanks to LA traffic a while back, probably will end up being more like nine hours instead of eight—and other than a few random clunking noises in Eric's Jeep when we left San Diego, things have been smooth sailing. Not only has the drive been beautiful along the coastal highway, but our banter and discussion over important subjects like whether Red Vines or Twizzlers are better have flowed—no sign of awkwardness, thank goodness. (And the answer is Twizzlers. As the middle school girl in me would say, *duh*.)

"I'm not sure. But I don't think it's good." Eric's right on that count, given the smoke now billowing from the hood of his Jeep.

"Eric!" I point.

"I see it, Shelby." He's super calm as he looks in his side mirror and moves to the right lane of the highway. Thankfully, there's a turnoff just ahead for some town named Hallmark Beach. The smoke clears a bit.

"Do you think it's safe to keep driving it?" My bare toes press into the Jeep's floorboard, so hard that my foot gets a Charlie horse. A tiny grunt issues from my lips as I flex it out.

Eric doesn't seem to notice. Not that I blame him since, you know, he's trying to keep us from dying. "We'll be fine. Can you get on your phone and look for a mechanic's shop or something? Might not be open at four o'clock on a Saturday, but you never know."

"Oh yeah. Of course." I fumble for my purse, which is sitting behind the center console, and grab my phone from inside. A few notifications catch my eye—Evie's texted about something and I want so badly to see if she's decided to finally budge on the gender reveal thing. But no, we've obviously got more pressing problems at the moment.

Once Eric's navigated safely off the highway and down the road just a tad, he pulls over, idling. "I'm afraid if I turn it off, it won't come back on." He crooks a grin. "Or it'll explode."

"Hilarious."

"Sorry." He lays his head back against the headrest, groaning. "This just stinks. We'll never make dinner with my uncle now."

"Oh no. You're right." My head pops up from the map on my phone, which is currently taking its dear sweet time with thinking. (It's been a while since we passed a large town and there's a good chance that the service out here is no good.)

Eric whips out his phone too and scans his own map. His service must be better than mine because pretty soon he points to his screen. "Here. Got something."

I lean across the divide between us and glance at his phone. Sure enough, there's a Burt's Auto on Main Street and the hours indicate it should be open for another hour. "You think we can make it?"

"Guess we'll find out. I'd hate to have to wait for a tow truck."

I'm quiet as he maneuvers slowly down the road, which veers under the highway and west toward the beach. Moments later, the town limits are within our sights—and it's adorable. The whole place. Multi-color pastel buildings line the main drag, and the shops all look occupied, vibrant, alive with people. Behind the row of the westernmost shops is the beach, the ocean, and on the eastern side of the roads, the shops back up to a forest of trees, a hill where houses sit.

A little way up, the road appears to be blockaded.

"Wonder what's going on there," I say. "Can we get to Burt's?"

Eric glances down at the screen of his phone and nods. "Looks like it's before that. Up here on the right." He pulls into a tiny parking lot and his Jeep gives one final heave before dying.

"What timing."

"Right?" Both hands on the wheel, Eric slumps his

head down against it. "Of all the times for Georgia to die on me …"

I want to laugh at the name he's given his vehicle, but he's clearly hurting. Now's not the time for a tease. "Don't worry. We're still going to meet your uncle. Maybe not tonight, but hopefully tomorrow."

He rolls his head sideways. "That does not look like an easy fix."

"But it might be."

"You're too optimistic for your own good, Shelby Phillips."

"I learn from the best." I unclip my buckle and slip on my flip-flops. "Now let's get out of this Jeep before it really does explode."

Shaking his head, Eric finally cracks another smile. "All right, you win. Come on."

We head into the shop, which is so tiny we are basically shoulder to shoulder in the waiting room until an older gentleman with wiry hair and a slightly bent back comes out to chat with us. His coveralls are stained with grease and his skin is so tan it's as leathery as my dad's wallet.

He flashes us a huge grin. "What can I do for you folks today? You must be here for the festival. Having rotten luck with your vehicle, and on such a special weekend too? That's a mighty shame. Oh, name's Burt Reynolds—but clearly I'm not the actor. Much more handsome, wouldn't you say?" He winks.

Eric's lips quiver as he glances at me, then back at Burt. "I'm Eric and this is Shelby. We're just passing through—or were, until my Jeep started smoking."

"Uh oh. That's a crying shame. Where ya headed?" The man doesn't bother to wait for an answer, though. Instead, Burt points to the door and we follow him out to the lot, where he makes himself at home and pops the Jeep's hood.

He sputters at the strong smell. "Woo-wee! That's a doozy. I remember the first time I—"

"Sorry, Mr. … Reynolds," Eric says. "It's just that, we're in a bit of a hurry. Do you think you can have this fixed quickly?"

"'Fraid not, son." Burt pulls off his glasses, attempts to clean them with his soiled sleeve, and puts them back on his face. "The missus is expecting me at the festival in one hour, sharp, and I have to get cleaned up first." He leans toward me, whispering in an exaggerated tone. "I don't exactly smell like a bucket of roses right now, do I?"

I can't help but feel endeared toward the man, even if what he's saying doesn't spell good news for Eric and me. "You smell lovely as far as I'm concerned."

"Well, ain't you the sweetest thing since coconut pie? You'd best be keeping this one, young man." He eyes Eric, who swallows hard and chuckles. But I know it's forced.

I fidget in my sandals. "What festival are you talking about?"

"Only the best darn food and wine festival this part of California has ever seen. Tourists come from all over the state to sample our local wares. And the best part? The event is free. You just have to pay for any samples you get." Burt's face brightens. "Y'all should come. I know my wife would love to meet a handsome young couple like yourselves."

"Oh, that's so sweet, but we really need to get going …" I trail off, because our full predicament is just hitting me. The look on Eric's face tells me he's already processed it, that I'm just slow. "When do you think you can have this fixed?"

"Well, now, that depends on what's wrong. I don't normally work Sundays, as it's the Lord's day, but I think God wouldn't have too much of a problem with me working tomorrow since it'd help you'uns out."

"Really?" Now it's Eric's turn to perk up. "That would be amazing. I can happily pay you extra for your time."

Burt waves a hand and bellows. "Nah, that's not necessary. You can pay me exactly what I'd normally charge." He checks the watch on his wrist. "But I do need to keep my word to the missus. Hmm."

"What is it, Burt?"

"Well." He strokes his bristly chin. "You'll be needing a place to stay, won't you? My sister-in-law runs the local inn."

"*The* local inn … as in, there's only one?" Eric asks.

"Mmm hmm. The Purple Seashell." Burt pulls a phone from his back pocket. "I know she was pretty booked up, but she might have something. I'd offer to let you stay with me, but our kids and their kids are visiting from out of town right now. House is full up."

Wow. What generosity, and from a complete stranger. "That's very sweet of you. Thank you for offering to contact her for us."

"Course, of course. Hang on just a second." Moving away, he lifts the phone to his ear.

I inch closer to Eric and take his hand, squeeze. "You doing okay?"

"This is disappointing, that's for sure." He looks down at our hands intertwined, back to my eyes. "But at least you're here with me. You have a way of keeping me calm."

My breath hitches and I bite my lip. "You always do the same for me."

Neither of us says anything else. We just continue to gaze at each other, and I remember Alexis's encouragement from earlier this week: *"Go on this trip with him and when the moment is right, you kiss that man again. Kiss him, and tell him you mean it."*

I've been turning the advice over and over in my mind. Can I really do it? Can I step out on the stage of life and risk everything for the possibility of love? What if I lose him? Now or later, doesn't matter. I can't stand the thought.

But I also can't stand the thought of never trying. Of forever wondering—what if?

"Shelbs—"

"Great news, you two!"

I start at the sound of the friendly mechanic walking back toward us and turn. "Oh, yeah?"

"My sister-in-law has one room available! There was a last-minute cancelation. It's like God himself was watching out for you."

"That's wonderful." Who knows what kind of shape this inn is in—Alexis has made me watch horror movies, and the small-town motels in those are almost never charming—but I'm grateful to have somewhere to stay tonight.

Beside me, Eric coughs. "Did you say *one* room?"

Oh.

I didn't even zero in on that part.

"Yup." Burt slaps his thigh. "And here's the kicker. It's the honeymoon suite, complete with a giant bed and a hot tub for two—just perfect for a couple of lovebirds like you. Guess some poor couple's flight got delayed after their wedding and they couldn't make it to their honeymoon. But their misfortune is your gain."

And now I know why they call this place *Hallmark Beach*. Because I've landed smack in the middle of an adorable little town and am about to be forced to share a room with my best friend, who I happen to love.

But who is also looking like he's swallowed something large and uncomfortable. Eric's cheeks are red and he can't stop coughing.

"Do you need some water?" I ask.

Burt just chuckles and slaps Eric on the back. "I think he's just speechless over the way things have worked out."

He's not the only one, Burt.

But maybe it's all a sign—the name of the town, the mechanic with connections to the one open room here, breaking down where we did. Maybe I'm being provided an opportunity to step out of the normalcy of the usual and imagine what life could be like if Eric and I *were* together.

Maybe it means it's finally time for that bravery Alexis talked about. "Thanks, Burt. We'll take it."

"We will?" Eric arches an eyebrow.

I squeeze his hand again. "Yes. We will."

"This place is swanky." Whistling, Eric turns a circle in our hotel room.

He's right. This is like nothing I've seen in horror movies—thank goodness—or what I'd expect from a place named The Purple Seashell (to be honest, I kind of thought we might find tacky *Little Mermaid* memorabilia everywhere). The high white ceiling boasts crisscrossing wooden beams. In one corner, there's a cozy brick fireplace with a few wingback chairs and a white rug resting in front of it, spread on the plushest carpet I think I've ever felt underneath my toes. The windows face the mountain and because we're on the top floor of the quaint inn, it feels like we're nestled in the trees. Happy early evening birdsong floats through the open window where I stand and run my fingers along the soft sheer pink curtains.

My eyes travel to the hot tub, situated on some tile right out in the open room next to the bathroom, which is sleek and comfortable without feeling overly modern.

And then there's the bed.

Burt's right—as a California King, it's ginormous. The rosy comforter is plump and soft (I tested it earlier while Eric used the restroom) and the headboard and rest of the furniture are painted and distressed to a white shabby chic.

And the mattress ... well, it's covered in pink rose petals.

As far as lovers' paradises go, this one would certainly rank at the top for me. It hits all the right spots—pink, plush, and perfect. Especially because of the guy I'm here with.

Of course, we aren't lovers. We're best friends.

For now. Maybe.

The thought brings a blush to my cheeks.

Eric catches me staring at the bed. "Um, I can take the rug." He removes his hat from his head, tosses it on the bedside table, and scratches behind his ear.

"Oh. Um." Wow, yeah, that's the clear elephant in the room. But he's got so much on his mind. This is not exactly a conversation we should be having in this moment. Not when he just had to call and postpone with his uncle, who sounded kind of perturbed, as if we had purposefully created car trouble for ourselves.

No, he doesn't need any other burdens—or heavy conversations—at the moment. So I smile. "Let's not worry about that right now. Right now, we are going to put all of our worries aside and go enjoy the Hallmark Beach Food and Wine Festival."

"I don't know, Shelbs." Eric plops onto the bed. "I just kind of want to stay in, order a pizza, and watch some TV."

I fully understand his sentiment. My comfy jammies are calling me and what he's describing sounds heavenly. Exactly my kind of night. But that's not what Eric needs right now.

Right now, more than anything, he needs a distraction.

"You? The king of fun, the guy who never lets me skip out on new experiences? No way." I grab his hand and tug until he's standing again. "Come on, Eric. I know this isn't what we had planned, but wouldn't you regret not getting out there?"

After one, two, three, his lips swing to the side in a smug smirk. "Who have you become, Miss Shelby? I do declare that you've changed." He's clearly imitating sweet Burt's accent—and doing it quite well, I might add.

But is what he's saying what he really thinks? My instinct is to withdraw, be hurt, because of what he said last week about me changing for a guy—for Rob. But you know what? No. If I've changed, then it's not for anyone but me. I'm becoming stronger, the person I've always wanted to be. Someone who can step outside of her comfort zone even when she's afraid.

Who maybe can even … I don't know. Flirt?

Biting my bottom lip, I step closer to him, lift on my tiptoes until my mouth is near his ear, and whisper, "I hope you like what you see." Then before I can tell if he's weirded out, I move away and grab my purse. "Now let's go."

"Yes, ma'am." He's on my heels and we head out the door and down the wooden stairs that squeak with each step.

The inn is a ghost town except for Burt's sister-in-law Janine at the front desk, a plump woman with graying hair cut in a bob. She glances up from her *People* magazine and waggles her fingers at us. "Ah, the love-birds. How did you find your accommodations?"

I glance at Eric, who has shifted uncomfortably every time someone has called us that—first Burt, then Janine at check-in.

And I find he's already looking at me, something new sparking to life in his eyes. "It's delightful, thank you, Janine." He's speaking to her, but his eyes don't leave mine.

A shiver tap dances up my spine.

Janine's giggles fill the lobby as she claps. "I'm surprised you came down so soon." She gives an exaggerated wink and okay, while it's kind of fun to pretend in my mind that Eric and I are on vacation together, to not correct people's assumptions, *that's* taking it a little too far.

I should tell her the truth. "Actually—"

"Actually." Eric is beside me in an instant and slips a hand around my waist. I freeze. "We can't wait to enjoy the accommodations further, but my girl here is starving and we've heard so much about your delightful festival that we had to check it out."

His girl? The mischievous glint is back in his eyes. Is this all a joke to him? Or is he taking advantage of the situation, of a chance to hold me like I've always wanted him to?

Maybe I'm not the only one who's been pretending in my mind.

"You're going to enjoy it. Be sure to stop by the

Loveland family's booth. Tell them Janine sent you and they'll give you a free glass of wine, on the house."

"That's very kind of you, Janine." Eric's fingers find one of the belt loops on my jeans and hook inside of it. "Any other tips?"

She takes a full five minutes to explain the best booths to get food, including the best chocolate mousse this side of the Rockies (her words, not mine). Meanwhile, I'm barely breathing because even though I'm used to Eric standing close to me, even putting his arm around me—this feels different.

And I like it. A lot.

Just when I think Janine is winding down her pitch, she snaps her fingers and leaps from her wheeled office chair, which flies backward and crashes into the wall. But she doesn't notice, just hustles off, yelling, "I've got just the thing."

"Friendly, isn't she?" Eric's breath is hot against my ear, and I nearly melt into the ground.

"Y-yeah. So friendly." Swallowing, I get the courage to look up at him—and the heat in his gaze scorches the very air hovering between us. Oh my. Every cell in my body tells me that this is *not* for Janine's benefit. That he wants this too.

And that gives me the extra courage to slink my arm around his waist and grab one of his belt loops too.

He grins and opens his mouth to speak when the woman gallops back, huffing and puffing and holding a blanket, a triumphant smile on her face. "Here. It's a perfect night for stargazing on the beach."

"Great idea, Janine," I manage.

It would be impolite to leave her standing there with an offering in her hand, but stepping forward unfortunately means I have to leave Eric behind. The decision is made for me, though. Eric's arm—the one that's holding me firm—lets go first, skating along my waist as he retracts it and reaches for the blanket. He bundles it in one arm and reaches for my hand with the other.

Janine shoos us out the door and into the night, where it's now dusk. A few blocks away, guitar music and jazzy singing drift from a small stage that's set up on the sand. (We saw it earlier when Burt gave us a ride to the inn.) Without saying a word, we head toward the festival and are upon it in minutes.

White tented booths line Main Street and a crowd swells around them. People here aren't in a hurry like in the big city (not that San Diego feels all that big, but it's much bigger than Hallmark Beach, population two thousand and twelve). They stop and chat, holding hands and sauntering while drinking from wine glasses and eating off tiny plates with little plastic forks and spoons.

And we join them. I visibly see the strain of this day melt from Eric's shoulders. He's such an extrovert, loves being around people—my exact opposite, but that's why we balance each other out so well. He buys me my favorite wine, a pinot from grapes grown locally, and feeds me some of his blueberry cake sample when my hands are full with the blanket and my glass.

"Mmm, wow. That reminds me of one my mom used to make."

His smile is soft and sweet as he takes his own bite,

finishing it off. "Yeah, that's really good. Hang on, okay?" He moves back to the booth where we got the cake. If I know him, he's going to buy a full slice this time.

While he's talking with the nice baker lady, I wander a bit to the edge of the festival, stepping out of my shoes and into the sand. It's cool and earthy against my toes, and I sigh at the familiar feeling. From not far away, the musician's soulful voice vibrates, so different from the music in my favorite shows, but still beautiful. The ocean undulates and slow dances to the joyful words couched in a mournful tune.

"There you are." Eric's beside me again and I look down at his hands, where he's holding his phone but no cake.

"What was that all about?"

He taps out something on his phone and clicks a final time. "Nothing much."

My phone vibrates in my back pocket. I narrow my eyes at him. "What did you do?" I shove the blanket into his hands, pull the phone from my pocket, and read the text he just sent me.

Marla's Blueberry Surprise.

My jaw drops. "It's a recipe."

"I had to beg and cajole, but old Marla finally budged and gave up her secret recipe."

"Eric, you didn't!" What had possessed him to do that?

He shrugs and puts his phone away. "I remember you saying once that your mom never wrote down any of her family's recipes. That you wish she had. So, this seemed like a decent second option."

And I don't care that I am holding a wine glass. I set it down in the sand, grab his and do likewise, and then launch myself at him, tucking my body into his and nearly toppling him in the process. "Thank you," I mumble against his chest.

"It wasn't that big of a deal." His heart is just under my ear and seems to pick up speed. Or maybe I'm hearing my own.

"Yes, it was. You've always seen me, Eric. Seen exactly the thing that would make me happiest."

Long moments skip by. Then, "I'm not sure I've always done that. But I want to from now on." He pulls back, and tucks my arm into the crook of his. "Come on. I see a great stargazing spot over there."

After we return our now-empty wine glasses to a server, we pick our way through the crowd down the beach quite a ways, where the people have thinned out and the sky has thickened up. By now it's fully embraced the twilight and Janine was correct—it's the perfect night for looking at stars.

Eric unfurls the blanket and lays it on the ground. Bits of sand fly up at the motion and we sit. The music of the night fills in the cracks of our silence until finally, he speaks. "I can't believe I'm really going to meet a family member. Maybe not tomorrow, but soon. Someone who shares my DNA, my blood. It's ..." Eric pushes out a breath and lies down, stretching out with one hand under his head. "I've wanted it for so long."

I pull my knees into my chest. "I know. I remember

what you said that night. The last time we went stargazing. Remember?"

"We saw that shooting star. Made a wish."

"And you wished that you would someday have someone in your life related by blood. That you would have a family of your own."

"And you wished to have your mom back."

I smile sadly. "An impossible wish." Then I give in to the pull to be near him and lie down beside him, my eyes fixed on the stars above.

"Sure, physically she's not here anymore, but I don't think it's as impossible as you think."

"What do you mean?"

"Just that I see her every day. In you."

I choke on a sob. "I want that to be true. So badly."

"It is. And that means you'd better find something else to wish for, because look." He points upward.

My eyes follow his finger and I gasp as a star graces the sky with a streaking light, leaving a trail of pixie dust in its wake. Squeezing my eyes shut for just a moment, I wish for bravery.

To tell Eric the truth.

Whatever may come.

When I open them, I angle slightly toward Eric, propping up my head with my hand. "Now it's certain your meeting with your uncle will go well."

"Why? Is that what you wished for?"

"No, but I figured that's what you did. It's what you've always wanted."

"Yeah, it definitely used to be." He pauses, and though it's dark, I sense his eyes on me. "Did I ever tell you that when I was nine—two years after my adoptive parents died—I was almost adopted again?"

"Really? No." But he wasn't. How awful for him.

"Yeah, it stunk. The adoption was nearly finalized and I was stoked to be part of a family again, this time with siblings. I had a foster brother, two sisters, all of them just a little younger than me. After being raised as an only child until that point, I craved that feeling of belonging, you know?"

"Of course you did." What child wouldn't? "What happened?"

"One night, I overheard my foster parents talking in the living room with my social worker. They said I was too moody—you know, because the only parents I'd ever known had died two years before that, go figure—and that it was affecting their 'real kids' negatively. And they just couldn't go through with it."

"Oh, Eric." I reach toward him and he places his hand in mine.

"Yeah, not so fun. It took about a week or so, but I was placed with another foster family. They gave me a really lame explanation for the canceled adoption—basically a 'it's not you, it's us' speech." He huffs out a sarcastic laugh. "But I knew the truth. No one wanted a kid around who was sad all the time."

"So you decided to be happy all the time instead."

"*Ding ding ding*. Bet you didn't know you were going to get a deep dive into Eric's psyche tonight, huh?"

"I'm sorry it happened to you, but I'm glad you told me." Without thinking, I bring his hand to my mouth and press a kiss there on his knuckles.

His fingers tighten around mine in response. "Here's the thing, though, Shelbs. When I met you—your family —I didn't have to pretend anymore. I just … fit. You all welcomed me whether I was blood or not. And I'd never felt that way before. Like I belonged."

"You do belong with us. With me."

Have I said too much? Not enough? But I can't be anything but real with him in this moment. He *does* belong with me. He always will, even if all we ever are is best friends. Once again, silence reigns between us, until Eric scoots his body closer to mine. "You know how I said having a family of my own is the thing I used to want more than anything?"

I have gone still, but manage a nod. "Yeah."

"It's not. Not anymore."

Ahhhhh. My heart is shuddering to a halt in my chest.

"And do you know what that thing is? The thing I want more than anything?"

I give the tiniest shake of my head. But I'm lying, because he's close enough now that I can see in his eyes what he's going to say—the thing I've always wanted to hear.

But I can't let him say it. Not before I speak my piece. "Eric, I can't have kids." The words rush from my mouth like a waterfall.

His forehead wrinkles. "What?"

I swallow, let go of his hand, and lie flat on the blanket again. Maybe this will be easier if I'm not looking at him, dim as it is out here. "What I mean is … I won't. I've got the gene. The one that means I could pass on my mom's disease to any biological kids I have."

"Oh. Wow, I'm sorry." A pause. "I'm not sure I understand why you're choosing to tell me this now."

Oh, goodness. I was wrong. He wasn't going to say that *I'm* the thing he wants more than anything. My cheeks are fire. "Um, well. I just ..." I shut my eyes. "Never mind." My voice squeaks.

"Shelbs."

I reopen my eyes, and he's even closer than before—still propped up on his elbow. "That doesn't matter to me."

And now I'm sure of it. We're talking about the same thing. On the same page. So I plow on, praying that I can communicate what's in my heart in a way he'll understand. "But it does. I know you want ..."

I can see enough to tell his mouth hangs open, as if realization has just dawned. In a flash, he's dropped back to the blanket, and his hand snakes around my waist, pulling me closer—so close. We are now facing each other, our bodies flush, and my hands find their natural place around his neck.

"Shelby Phillips, there is nothing that I want more in this life than *you*."

He waits, probably for me to say something, but my mouth is complete cotton and I think it's possible that my stomach is now residing in my toes.

Did he say what I think he just said? But ... "You have always wanted a family."

"I have one right here, with you. Remember?"

The ocean laps and an owl hoots somewhere in the

distance. The distant chatter of people, the music from the festival, they are all drowned out by the power of this moment between two people. Only he and I exist.

"So that kiss on Tuesday?"

"It was real for me," he whispers. "So real."

Never has there been a moment in any musical sweeter than this. It's better than Fiyero helping Elphaba fake her own death. Better than Satine singing Christian their secret song in front of a full audience. And even better than Raoul rushing to rescue Christine from the Phantom.

Because this, right here, is reality. *My* reality.

And I can't do it anymore. Can't hold back the longing in my soul. Can't hold back my heart from him. He is all I want, and it's been a long time coming.

Maybe this … this is true bravery.

So I finally let go of the fear—that I'm doing something wrong, unkind, by fanning this spark between us into a flame, a fire—and embrace … well, him.

Though it doesn't seem possible, I pull him nearer. "It was real for me too."

With the stars as our witness, I give Eric my heart, along with a kiss I hope he'll never forget.

I know I never will.

thirteen

. . .

YOU KNOW how some people say that in the light of day, what happened in the night can look like a mistake?

I don't feel that way. At all.

In fact, it almost feels like today is the start of the rest of our lives. And it's beginning in the best way possible, with breakfast in bed. Okay, not technically in bed. Rather, on the big rug by the fireplace, where Eric and I sit on the ground, propped up against pillows and a couple of wingback chairs.

I take one final bite of toast and push aside the tray Eric found outside our door this morning with a note from Janine saying to enjoy. "That was amazing."

Next to me, Eric has already polished off his entire omelet, slice of toast, bacon, and fruit. He takes a sip of coffee from his white mug, ahhing when he's done. "Yes, it was." Setting the coffee on the side table between the two chairs, he looks at me. His hair is standing on end every which way and his T-shirt is rumpled from the hours we sat here talking last night after coming in from the festival.

Eventually we grew tired and I crawled into the big bed all by myself. Despite my protests, Eric stayed on the rug, saying his good judgment was all worn out—and that made me love him all the more. I think we finally fell asleep sometime around five am and didn't wake up until a call woke us just after ten. When Eric looked at his phone, it turned out he'd missed more than just the one.

The first call: Eric's apartment superintendent, letting him know they finally have an apartment ready for him.

The next: Burt, telling us he got in early today and should have Eric's Jeep "right as rain" by eleven.

And finally: Eric's uncle, saying that he is driving down to Hallmark Beach because today was his only chance to see Eric, as he's leaving the country tomorrow for a long trip. We're meeting him for lunch in a few hours before we head back to San Diego.

"Do you know what is even more amazing than that food?" Eric smooths a hand through his hair, which only makes it more crazy and adorable.

Despite my polka dot pajama pants and the fire we've got going in the grate, my legs grow chilly so I tug a blanket over them. "What?"

"That I get to do this." Then he lunges for me.

I squeal and try to hide under the blanket, but he catches me and covers my lips, my cheeks, my neck in kisses. "I'm not awake enough for this!" Grabbing the pillow from behind me, I try to smack him with it, but he's persistent. Finally, I give in and kiss him back, full and long.

This is all my dreams, coming to fruition.

He catches my bottom lip gently between his teeth, gives a little tug, swoops in for a final kiss, then falls back against his pillow, his breathing as rough as mine. "Do you know how long I've wanted to do that?"

"No." I press my fingertips against my cheeks to cool my face. "How long?"

"Since senior year of high school."

Ah. "Just before prom?"

He nods and draws me against his chest as he looks at the fireplace. "One day in the locker room, I over-heard Channing DePri telling Lucas Walker that he was going to ask you to prom."

"Channing? Seriously? I didn't even think he knew I existed." After all, I was just a mousy girl in the corner and he was the big football star.

"Uh, every guy knew you existed, Shelbs. You were —and still are—beautiful, but you were—and still are— different than other girls. You actually care about people, and that makes your beauty shine through a thousand times more than those girls who only care about how many calories they eat or how expensive their jeans are."

There's something super wrong with his theory, unfortunately. "If that's true, why was Trevor the only guy who ever asked me out?"

Eric is silent for a moment and it draws me backward a bit so I can look at him. Finally, "I may have told everyone to keep their paws off of you."

"What? Why? Because you liked me?" That doesn't sound like Eric. He's not really the jealous type.

"No. Well, maybe. I actually didn't realize it until I overheard Channing's plan. Trevor was the only dude who didn't listen to my warnings to stay away." His eyes beg me for forgiveness. "I thought I was protecting you, you know? High school guys are crummy. Believe me, they were not worthy of you."

"I suppose I should feel grateful to you then."

"Was that sarcasm I detect?"

"Maybe." I stick my tongue out at him before sobering. "I just spent so many years wondering if I would always be invisible. Sometimes I thought Mom was the only one who ever really saw me. And then she was gone."

"I always saw you—how could I not? But it took my stupid teenage brain a hot minute to see you in *that* way."

"And then you did, and my brother scared you off."

"Yeah, plus I knew *I* didn't deserve you any more than Channing or any of his idiotic pals. But I worked hard, made something of myself—even if that something is just a lowly history teacher."

I love his teasing voice. Always have. "Well, I'm a lowly kindergarten teacher, so there." I curl into him again. "I don't need much. Just you. And you've always been good enough for me."

"I knew better, and so did Cody that day he warned me off."

"I kind of want to be mad at him."

"Nah. He was just being a good older brother. Protective."

"Plus, he didn't want to lose you," I say. "To be honest, he probably would have. Much as it would have killed me, I'd have broken up with you once I got my DNA test results."

He kisses my hair. "I wish you would have told me, Shelby."

"I didn't know how. Didn't think I could tell you without …" I swallow. "Without revealing how I felt about you. And then I was afraid I'd be too weak to resist you if there was even the remote possibility that you liked me back."

"But see, that's the thing. I wish you'd given me a chance, you know? To communicate, talk it through. We're usually pretty good at that. At least, I thought we were."

I'm quiet for a while, my fingers running up and down his corded forearm that's wrapped around my middle. "I've always been fully honest about everything else, but when it came to how I felt about you, I just …" Angling my face upward, I look at him.

"You just what?" He leans down and kisses me again, and I realize how blessed I am that this man would want me, even after what I told him last night. Realize that I was more afraid than I knew of being rejected for something that was never my fault—my genetics.

And the fact that he wants to be with me in spite of it makes me love him all the more.

I sigh. "I wanted to do the right thing. If my mom had known about her disease beforehand, I'm certain she would have made the same decision I am about not having kids. My mom was the best woman I knew, and so that's what I have to do. But if it meant hurting you, meant you couldn't have what you want … a family. I mean, not that we're getting married or anything yet. Or at all. I just …" Oy, I'm botching this. My eyes fall.

"Hey." He tips my chin upward again and kisses my nose. "I told you. You have been my family since the day we met."

"I know, but you always wanted that genetic connection."

"Right. And now we don't have to worry about that, remember?"

Yes, his uncle. "But what if it goes poorly when you finally do meet up? I don't think it will because you're awesome and anyone would be lucky to know you, but …" Am I being insensitive to ask this?

"I've thought about it, believe me. But none of that changes how I feel about you or what we can build together if we try."

Speaking of how he feels about me … "So if you've liked me all these years—"

"Why did I finally decide to act on it?" At my nod, he angles in, kisses me sweetly. "Seeing that Rob guy all over you when you were dancing … yeah. Something in me just snapped. It was bad enough being near you every day, smelling your coconut shampoo—which drives me wild, by the way—and only being able to hold you casually, as a friend. But having another guy try to swoop in and take you?"

"I'm sensing a pattern with you," I tease.

"Right? It sounds so archaic and caveman, huh? Spurred on only when I'm jealous of another guy. But I hope you know that's not what this is. It's not like some possessive jealousy that's unhealthy or whatever."

"I don't think that." Because I know Eric's heart, and he's not that guy.

"I think it just really made me realize that if I didn't say something, do something to make you see me in another light, then I might really lose you to another guy. And this time, unlike some high school relationship, it might be forever. For all I know, you could have fallen in love with Rob, married him."

"You had no reason to be jealous of Rob. He doesn't hold a candle to you."

"Which only shows you have terrible taste in men."

"Whatever. I have the best." I pause, thinking of the timeline Eric has established for me. "So, wait. You decided to try to change things right after the dancing incident—"

"Which will henceforth be known as Dance-Gate."

I laugh. "Right. So that means ..." I narrow my eyes. "Wait, was the 'no shirt on while making eggs' incident before or after Dance-Gate?"

"Ahhh, Shirt-Gate."

I roll my eyes. "Sure. Shirt-Gate."

Chuckling, he flexes his bicep. "Shirt-Gate was actually before Dance-Gate. But it was the first time I thought I might honestly stand a chance with you. That you might feel the same way about me as I did about you."

My cheeks flame. "Why?"

"Because your eyes told me you were hungry that morning—and not just for eggs."

I groan and twist away from him, burying my face in my hands. "Excuse me while I go die now." My palms muffle my voice.

"No one can blame you." Clearly he has no problem understanding my mumbling. "I *am* a hunky beefcake."

I turn back and punch him playfully. "No one says beefcake anymore." But then I tug at the hem of his T-shirt. "But I will admit, I don't *hate* your abs."

Eric holds up his arms as if he's just scored a goal. "And that, ladies and gentlemen, is how it's done."

"You're ridiculous." I strain for a glimpse of the clock way over on the table beside the bed. "As much as I wish we could stay here forever—"

"Why don't we? We don't have to meet my uncle for another few hours. And we could just come back here after instead of driving home. Make a vacation out of it. I don't want to go back to reality."

"That does sound tempting. Except there's rehearsal tomorrow."

"I don't have to be there. My sets are done."

"Well, I do." And the reminder is enough to kick me off the high of this weekend, of this time with Eric. Shouldn't admitting our feelings make me feel better about everything else in my life? Where are the rose-colored glasses I've heard so much about?

"Ah yes. You're the star after all."

"Don't remind me."

He picks up my hand, brings it to his lips, kisses it. "You're still nervous."

"Of course I am. I started off nervous, kind of got a little more confident in between." I set a hand on my stomach. "But when I think about performing in two weeks, I kind of want to barf."

"That's normal. Nerves. Stage fright. Especially after what happened when you were younger. But don't let fear creep in and take over. You're stronger now, Shelbs. I've never seen you so strong, so confident in yourself."

"You've been my rock, Eric. I couldn't do this without you."

"Yes, you could." He pulls me to himself once more, cocooning me in the safety of his embrace. Here there are no stages, no worries over legacies or living up to the dreams we have for ourselves. There is only him and me, and that is enough. It will always be enough. "But you don't have to."

The longer I spend in this cute little town, the more I love it.

"We definitely need to come back here sometime." While keeping hold of Eric's hand, I peek inside the window of a shop that sells flavor-infused olive oils. As someone exits, I sniff and come away heady with the gorgeous aromas filtering outside.

"It sure is a little piece of heaven, isn't it?" Eric stops and pulls me to him, smiling. "I think I might be partial to it just because of what happened here."

"You mean meeting your uncle?" It hasn't happened yet, of course—we're on our way to the little diner now to eat lunch with him.

"That, sure. But I was talking more about this." He reaches for me, skims the back of my neck with his fingers as he tilts my head upward and bends to kiss me.

Happy sigh. I could do this all day.

"Oh. That. Yeah, I guess that's been all right."

Eric fists his hand and pummels it right against his chest, as if he's been stabbed. "You wound me, Shelbs."

"Well, that just won't do." I take his hand in my own, turn it over, and examine it before pressing a kiss into his palm. Then my eyes meet his. "Guess I'll have to figure out a way to make it up to you."

His hands slip around my waist. "I might have some suggestions." Then he tugs me into the space between the olive oil shop and the bookstore, where a narrow path that's currently deserted leads out to the beach. The rays of the midday sun are hidden from this space, where the buildings shadow much of the walkway.

It's ridiculous, because it's not like kissing Eric is forbidden or that we're hiding from anyone or ashamed of our newfound relationship, but I imagine this is what it would have felt like to hide beneath the bleachers with a boy just before kissing him. The emotions I'm riding are hopefully more mature than that, but I still can't help but giggle at the thought. It's high-pitched and far too reminiscent of a high schooler, but at the moment, I don't care.

For the first time, I'm in love—and the man I love likes me back. The way he looks at me, with adoration in his eyes, like he needs me and wants me and never wants to be away from me …

It's mind-blowing and breathtaking and that means I can't think or inhale. I can only give in to the siren of his kiss.

He gently nudges me up against the tucked-away wall and places a palm above my head, leaning in with one arm to support him. Then Eric gives me a lesson in patience as he lowers his mouth slowly toward mine, hovering there before turning his attention first to my jawline. His ministrations are slow and steady and I don't know whether to tell him to slow down or hurry up so my lips can enjoy the same pleasure.

While his lips stake their sensuous claim, my fingers grasp for his belt loops and tug him closer. He complies with my unspoken but forceful request and I am tenderly pinned between him and the wall.

But I am not a prisoner. Even if I was, I'd have no wish to be free.

My hand finds one of his. When he leans in to ensure that my neck is not left out of this loving exchange between his mouth and my body, our joined hands end up clasped above my head. Just as I think that my knees might give out from the blitz of adrenaline, my patience is eventually rewarded when Eric drags his kiss straight to my lips.

And this time, there's nothing slow or steady about

it. There is no hesitancy, no playfulness, only the pure longing and passion of years poured out into minutes. It's like one of those vacuum-sealed bags of clothing when the plug is removed and all the air can finally rush into the hidden places.

We are making up for lost time.

All these years, I feared it might be slightly strange to kiss my best friend. But it's only strange if "strange" is a synonym for "perfect," "amazing," or "completely incandescent."

My whole body buzzes with endorphins and somewhere in the back of my mind, the thought of an upcoming something keeps flitting in and out while Eric kisses me.

Oh! Right. "Eric," I manage. "Your uncle."

He groans, his eyes hazy and liquid sapphires. "Do we have to?" Straightening a bit, he rubs one of my tank top straps with his thumb.

"The man is driving all this way to meet you."

"I know. You're right. As always."

"Can I get that in writing?" I smile, tilt my head. "Don't worry. We can pick up where we left off after our meeting."

"Can I get *that* in writing?" He grins and I shake my head at him. Then he sobers, blows out a breath. "I'm nervous, Shelbs."

I step away from the wall, brushing at my backside in case there's any sand lingering there. "It's going to be great. I'll be there the whole time if you want me to be."

"I do." Exhaling, he nods and reaches for my hand again. "Let's go."

As we step out of the alleyway, a few middle-aged women stroll toward us and smile knowingly before power-walking past. My neck heats as we make our way to The Green Robin, an adorable restaurant with lots of outdoor seating. I'm rather partial to the rosy-colored walls, and the yellow-and-white striped awnings that hover over tables with bright green chairs just make me smile.

Despite the well-spent delay in our arrival, we're still a few minutes early. The hostess leads us to a table situated on the outdoor patio facing the beach. About a half-mile down, a pier stretches out into the ocean. The boardwalk abutting the patio bustles with dog walkers, stroller pushers, cyclists, and runners, and the diner is hopping. Good thing Janine suggested we get a reservation this morning or we'd be waiting for a while.

As soon as we sit next to each other on one side of the table, Eric grabs a menu from the center and scans it, then closes it, sets it down, picks it up, opens it again. Leaning against his strong shoulder, I place my hand on his knee and squeeze. Wordlessly, he turns his head and kisses my temple, and his body relaxes.

I open my menu and we peruse it together, pointing out a few items before our server approaches the table. Unlike the infamous Gwen from the Italian restaurant with my friends, this woman—who I guesstimate to be in her late twenties or early thirties—is wearing an open expression, jeans, a white blouse, and pink Keds. From her high cheekbones to her long blonde hair pulled back into a casual pony, she strikes me as the kind of girl I'd love to be friends with.

"Hey, y'all," she says in a slight Southern accent. I didn't know so many Southerners lived in this small coastal town. "Welcome to The Green Robin. My name's Lucy and I'd love to get you something delicious to drink. We're still serving mimosas if that interests you—breakfast food all day on Sundays."

"Oh, that sounds good, but I'll be driving," Eric says.

Lucy puts her hand on her hip, flipping her tiny notepad up in the process. "Are y'all by chance Eric and Shelby, the nice young couple my Uncle Burt helped with their car?"

I smile and lean across the table so I can see her a bit better. "We are. Your uncle is the sweetest man."

"I know. He and my aunt took me in when I was sixteen. Best people I know." Lucy looks like she wants to say more, but then laughs and shakes her head. "But you didn't come here to hear my sad story. If you're looking for an upgrade from water, I'd try the strawberry lemonade. It's to die for. Trust me."

"Sure," says Eric.

"Sounds great. And we'd like straws too, please." I close the menu. "We're waiting on one more, so we'll order once he's here."

"No problem. I'll be back in a bit with those drinks." She pivots and leaves, her steps bouncing her hair as she goes.

And, coming from the opposite direction, is a man who is the spitting image of Eric. Or maybe Eric is the spitting image of him? Either way, they're definitely related. Dan Jenkins is of course older and also more polished looking in his tan chino shorts, polo shirt, and boat shoes than Eric's usual fare of board shorts, a T-shirt, and that Padres hat. For a man in his fifties, he's super fit and his brown hair has hardly any gray hair. I wonder if he dyes it?

Eric has yet to notice him, so I inhale and squeeze his knee again. He looks up from the menu he's studying and his body freezes.

"Breathe," I whisper, just before the man reaches our table.

"Eric?" he asks, slight hesitation in his voice.

"Y-yes. Yes." Eric stands and holds out his hand. "Good to meet you, Dan."

"You too." Dan takes Eric's hand and gives it a firm shake before lowering himself into the seat across from Eric, whose jaw is slack.

For the first time since I've met him, he's speechless.

My fingers drum Eric's knee and he covers my hand with his own, squeezing hard. I clear my throat. "I'm Shelby, Eric's ..."

"Girlfriend."

My gaze crashes into Eric's and settles there as a smile twitches on my lips. "Yeah, girlfriend." Then I turn back to Dan, who is glancing between us. "Thanks for making the drive down."

"Yeah." The word rushes from Eric. "Thank you."

The two men just stare at each other, maybe assessing each other? Or maybe just not knowing quite what to say. Dan shifts in his seat and picks up a menu.

We spend the next few long minutes in silence as we each look over the menu. I decide rather quickly on a club sandwich on a homemade croissant—because hi, that sounds amazing—just in time for Lucy to come back with our drinks, including a water for Dan. She takes our order and leaves us to once again fill the silence.

"So what do you do, Dan?" I ask.

"I'm an attorney."

Ah, that would explain the pressed shirt and the short hair.

"I was in the military before that. Stationed all over the world." He grabs a straw and pokes the plastic out through the paper. "That's where I was when your mom ..." He clears his throat, looks down at the table. His unreadable expression becomes very readable, and what I see there breaks my heart.

Regret.

"Did you ..." Eric's teeth click together. "Did you know about me?"

"No." Dan shoves the straw into his glass, splashing a bit of water over the sides. "We were estranged and our parents were already gone. There was no one left to tell me she'd passed. By the time I got back state-side and decided to look for her, I found her grave instead."

When Eric doesn't say a word, I jump in. "That must have been really hard. I'm sorry."

"Honestly? I was almost desensitized to loss at that point. Took a lot of therapy to get right after the things I saw in the Marines." He scratches his chin, which is completely clean-shaven, and focuses on Eric. "I admit, after I got your email, part of me doubted you were Sheila's kid. Those DNA tests aren't always right, you know. But seeing you ... well, you've got her eyes. Her nose. *My* nose." Shaking his head, he blows loose a half breath. "It's a little bit surreal."

"Tell me about it. I thought I was all alone in the world." His fingers thread through mine. "As far as my blood relations go, anyway."

Be still my heart. If I have anything to say about it, Uncle Dan is getting invited to every family function and Eric will never be alone again.

"I got used to being alone." Dan fiddles with his straw, swirling the ice in his glass. "Not sure I know how to be a family man. I travel a lot. Leave the country quite often. Tomorrow I'm heading to Switzerland for work. Next month, it's Prague. The fact you caught me in between trips is actually kind of a miracle."

Oh.

I try to get a bead on whether this is disappointing news to Eric. But he only dives into asking Dan about his travels, and that gets the conversation spinning. When Lucy brings us our food, we dig in and keep chatting until it's been two hours and we really need to get on the road if we're going to make it home tonight.

We all stand and walk through the diner and out onto Main Street. Eric's Jeep is still sitting in Burt's lot, but Dan takes out his keys and hits his key fob. A red Miata beeps a few feet away.

Dan turns to us. "Well, thanks for contacting me. I'm not sure when I'll be free again, but maybe we could find some time during the holidays."

The holidays? But Thanksgiving is still four months away.

However, Eric doesn't seem put off by this suggestion. He simply reaches out a hand again. "Sounds like a plan." Once they shake hands, Dan climbs into his car and drives off, and Eric takes my hand and tugs me down Main Street. There's a bounce in his step and he's grinning. "That was crazy awesome."

I bite my lip, nod. "I'm glad it worked out to meet up. He seems really nice." Our stroll is slow-going thanks to the late-afternoon crowd. For such a small town, there sure are a lot of people. I'm guessing many of them are tourists like us, here to enjoy the quaint atmosphere and gorgeous weather. But at this rate, we won't be getting home till after midnight.

"Yeah, he's great, isn't he? World traveler, a Marine, upstanding citizen." Eric comes to the edge of a crosswalk, looks both ways, and starts to cross the street with me in tow. "I can't believe I have someone who looks like me. He even sounded like me. Did you notice that?"

His good humor is infectious. "I did, actually." Of course, there were many differences between Eric and Dan, but if he's choosing to marvel at the similarities, I'm all for it.

We're in the middle of the crosswalk, but apparently Eric doesn't care about that. He stops, picks me up, and spins me around, then plants a kiss on my lips. Several horns honk, but I don't get the impression that they're mad since a few hoots and hollers accompany them. Still, I have no wish to get run over and, laughing, I pull away from Eric and run to the other side.

He catches me quickly and tickles me before I place my arms around his neck. "It's so good to see you happy," I say.

"Of course I'm happy. More than happy. Other than being with you, meeting someone who shares my blood is the greatest high I've ever experienced." He hoots. "It's addicting."

I freeze. What does he mean by that? "Addicting?"

"Yeah. It's one of the best feelings in the world."

My hands fall from around his neck just like my heart is falling splat on the sidewalk. "Addiction implies that you want to feel this way over and over again."

"Yeah …? So?"

I poke my tongue into my cheek. "So, Dan seems very busy. As in, you probably won't see very much of him over the years."

Eric sticks his hands into his pockets. "Way to kill the mood, Shelbs."

"I didn't mean …" The concrete beneath my feet is suddenly very interesting. A small crack spiderwebs outward. If it isn't treated, isn't smoothed out, that small crack will eventually grow and compromise the integrity of this entire section of sidewalk. It would make the path impassable. "I'm just saying, that being with Dan might not truly satisfy your new addiction."

"K, Shelbs, I normally pride myself on being able to read your mind, but you're gonna have to spell this out for me. What in the world are you talking about?"

Isn't it as obvious to him as it is to me? "The only logical way to feed that high you experienced is to be near your family all the time. Which, in your case, would mean having kids. Your biological kids, Eric." I barely choke out the last words before heartburn takes over, scalding my chest.

He groans. "Shelby." Eric's in front of me in an instant, and I'm in his arms again even faster. "That's not what I meant."

"But—"

"Look. I'll be honest. Would I love to have children that look like me, sound like me, maybe even act like me—except for the really annoying parts, that is?" He quirks a smile. "Yes, absolutely."

I shudder. But I'm glad he's being honest.

"But"—he continues—"if that 'addiction,' as you call it, means I don't get you, then I'll give it up. Cold turkey."

"That's not fair to you." And I'm right back to the place where we started in all of this—except now, I know what it feels like for Eric to hold me in his arms. I know what it's like to see him excited to experience his dream too.

How are we ever to choose the thing that's right for us both?

"You know what isn't fair? That I get to date the most beautiful, caring, amazing woman I've ever known when I'm such a mess." His finger skims my cheek. "I'm really glad life isn't fair."

"Eric." Despite his sweet words, I frown. "I don't know how to reconcile this."

"You don't have to know everything right now. Neither of us does. Can you just trust me to know my own heart? You just focus on what it is *you* want—because all *I* want is for you to be happy." He leans in close.

"I don't know how to do that," I whisper against his lips.

"One step at a time, beautiful."

Okay. I can do that. I think.

"One step at a time." And in that moment, I make a promise to myself.

I will shove this doubt from my mind.

And to prove it, I seal that promise with a kiss.

fourteen

. . .

IT'S BEEN NEARLY a week since Eric and I officially became a we.

Nearly a week of stolen kisses, of dates—watching movies, eating out, taking walks along the Bay. Things we've done a thousand times together that now have new meaning.

Nearly a week of being teased by my friends and roommates, including Lauren, who returned from Kentonia the same night that Eric and I did from Hall-mark Beach, a ring on her finger (which surprised exactly none of us!).

Nearly a week of Eric continuing to help me be brave as it regards the musical. Thankfully, rehearsals this week seemed to go more smoothly. I've told Rob that I'm dating Eric now, and he said that he suspected I might be. We've worked out how to stage kiss without it being overly weird, and now I just have to ignore the fact that the show opens in one week.

How much life has changed in nearly a week.

It's even stranger now, because instead of our normal girls' night out, I'm standing inside a large-chain baby store with my best girlfriends in the world. Kayla is back to her normal, feisty, non-crying self—*"Thank the Force for the second trimester!"*—albeit with a tiny bump on her belly, and Evie is simply glowing now that she can eat again.

Both of them are holding those little red registry scan guns, pointing and clicking at anything that looks remotely like something they might need. Evie has clicked lots of blue clothing, Kayla lots of pink and purple (yeah, Evie finally told us she's having a boy and Kayla's having a girl—apparently they're already planning their kids' wedding so they can be in-laws someday).

Since none of us has children, we aren't much help with selecting products to put on their registries, although I did ask my sister for some advice before coming. Deb texted me some brands to steer clear of, what she likes best, and a few items that apparently are "professional mom approved."

"According to this"—I glance down at my phone as we navigate the feeding aisle—"Deb thinks the Medela brand is the highest quality pump but likes the Dr. Brown's bottles best. Although she did concede that every baby is different." I smile, remembering how she went through ten different bottles before my nephew Barrett settled on one he liked. Who knew babies were so picky?

"Hard to believe that we are going to be able to feed

our children with milk our bodies produce." Evie's voice is hushed, awed, as she touches a breast pump on display. "Nature is incredible."

"Yes, so incredible that we're gonna have to get hooked up to one of these every day like cows." Leave it to Kayla, who picks up a box of breast pump parts and moos before wrinkling her nose.

Evie elbows her playfully, then scans several items with her gun. Her free hand naturally finds its way to her stomach before urging Kayla and Alexis down the aisle to help her look for a specific pacifier her mother told her about. Apparently she loved it as a baby.

It may seem ridiculous, given the fact we've been here for at least an hour, but in that gentle movement—Evie setting her hand on her growing belly—my heart drops. Instead of hurrying along, going with the flow of where my friends direct, I take a moment to really look at where I am.

Surrounded by things I might never buy for myself.

Breast pump parts? Do adoptive moms have any use for that? And I definitely won't need the stretch mark cream or pregnancy pillow we passed ten minutes ago.

Hot tears poke the back of my eyes and I swipe at the few that spring out. Ugh. Why is this hitting me so hard right now? I've had years to come to terms with my decision to not have biological children.

And yet, being here, in a store that smells of baby powder and citrus, filled to the brim with things geared toward moms who have nine months to prepare for a birth, I want nothing more than to crawl under one of the shelves. Of course, that would be gross, but walking out the automatic door into the Friday evening air sounds like a fabulous option.

"What's wrong, Shelbs?" Lauren appears at my elbow.

When I don't speak, she wraps an arm around my waist and lets me lay my head on her shoulder. But this leaves me staring directly at the breast pump, so I step away and turn. "I'm okay."

And I am. I've got wonderful friends, a great family, a career I love, a chance to redeem myself onstage … and a man who supports me. Who maybe will someday love me the way I love him, if he doesn't already.

Just because I can't have a biological child doesn't mean my life is less than.

Right? Totally. Definitely.

And yet …

"Is everything good with Eric?"

We start walking to catch up with the others, who are making lots of noise from several aisles over. I can practically hear Alexis's rolled eyes from where we are as Kayla talks about why she wants to use cloth diapers.

"More then. He's amazing." My lips tick up at the corners. Thinking about him puts a silver lining on any bad day.

"You seem really happy."

I loop my arm through hers as we meander through a whole aisle filled with blankets of varying sizes. "I'm not the only one. I still can't believe you're marrying a prince. You're gonna be Princess Lauren."

"Technically, I'll be a duchess, but yeah. Who would have thought? It's so weird." She's beaming as her eyes take in the store. "You know what's even weirder? Thinking about having kids with him." Her cheeks redden. "I mean, not thinking about … *that*. That's not weird. That sounds wonderful."

I laugh. "I totally understand." And I do. The thought of being intimate with Eric one day has my toes tingling and stomach buzzing. It's something I thought I'd be scared of—you know, having only ever kissed one other guy in my entire life—and while, sure, there's some apprehension about the unknown, I'm actually quite comfortable with the idea of taking that step when the timing is right.

We round the corner, our shoes squeaking on the linoleum.

Lauren continues. "What I mean is, it's weird to think that I'll be raising a future king or queen. Princes and princesses." She blows out a breath. "And as lovely as Kentonia is, it's weird to think about not living here, with you all. You're my people."

Taking her hand in mine, I stop walking. "And we always will be. But you have Topher, and that's all that matters."

"True, I have him, and I love him, but he can't be everything to me. I'm figuring out that there's got to be something beyond him—beyond any one person, really. Otherwise, when he inevitably fails to live up to the standard I have in my head of what he should be or how he should act, my whole world will fall apart."

"That's a really good point." For so long, Eric has been my person. But what if he and I don't work out? Or, God forbid, what if something happened to him? I have to be able to exist outside of him too. "So you're saying all of your fears and worries don't automatically disappear just because you're with the man you love?"

I say it playfully, but in that moment, I realize that I've been imagining they would. Which is ridiculous. Yet I've been so focused on the wonder of what would happen if Eric and I were to ever be together, that I never pictured the rest. All the trials we would face.

Including not having biological kids. We haven't talked about it since last Sunday, but all the uncertainty, the emotions, of our conversation, bubble to the surface now.

"Not even close, sister. But Topher does give me a safe place to land when I get really anxious or scared. And I hope I do that for him too." She tilts her head, squeezes my hand. "It's hard for you to be here, huh?"

How does she know?

"You don't have to pretend with me. With any of us. I'm sure Kayla and Evie would understand if you left."

I shake my head. "I couldn't do that to them. They're my friends. I want to support them. And I *am* excited for them."

"You're allowed to be both, you know. Excited for them, and sad for yourself."

"There's no point in feeling sad for myself, though."

"Emotions don't have to have a point. And you can't always talk yourself out of them."

"When did you get so wise?" I sniffle as the tears come again and I turn toward one of the blankets. Pulling it off the shelf, I hold it up to my face and it's the softest material I've ever felt. That should be comforting, but it only serves to remind me that I won't ever be swaddling a baby that I carried for nine months. Even if Eric and I get married, there will never be babies crawling around who are a combination of both me and him.

"I'm not that wise. But I am learning and growing, and so are you." Lauren pauses. "Shelby, I'm going to ask you something, and please don't be mad at me. But I know I'd have never learned some of the things I did if you and others hadn't challenged my thinking."

I peek up at her, nod my permission to continue.

"Is the no kids thing absolutely off the table? I mean, I know you think your mom never would have had them in your situation, with the knowledge you have now about your genetics, but does the fact you have the gene mean that you will for sure pass the disease on to your kids?"

"Well, no." I swallow. "But there's a chance."

"There's also a chance we'll get into a car accident on the way home today. Does that mean we shouldn't drive a car?"

I pull my arms up, around my chest, hugging the blanket there. I don't care if it's for babies—it's totally coming home with me. "That's kind of an extreme example."

"Is it, though? As an eighteen-year-old, you made a decision with the facts you had available to you then, but have you really discussed this decision with anyone?"

"Eric and I discussed it."

"I don't mean that you told him how it would be. I

mean, have you had a real discussion? Like, with an open mind?"

"I guess not." And, ouch, that hurts to say.

"Okay. And what did Eric say when you told him your decision?"

"That it didn't matter to him. That he has a family, and it's me."

"I knew I liked that guy for a reason." Lauren picks up a tiny stuffed elephant and turns it over in her hand absently, stroking the silky ears. "I'm sure he meant it too. But if you guys end up together, then you should make a decision together."

Her words make sense, but they also cut a hole in the fabric of what I've always known to be true. Hope seems to wave at me from the other side, but what if it's actually death disguised as hope? "I can't change my genetics."

"Of course not. You can't change your genetics any more than I can change the fact that Topher is a prince. And Eric has to accept that about you just like I accepted Topher. Because I love him." She sets the elephant back in the bin with a slew of other animals, then fixes her sensitive brown eyes on me. "But he was very stuck in how he'd always done things. Didn't think there was any other way. At first, I thought I had to just accept those ways as part of his life too, or I'd lose him. However, once we started talking through those issues —really talking about them—it turned out there were other options for handling things."

Hope's now beckoning, crooking its finger, asking me to step through the hole, into a new world of light.

But what if that light goes out the moment I do? Or worse—years later?

Oh, how I wish Mom was here. She'd give me the strength to make the decision she would have if she'd had the pre-knowledge I did. To help me be brave and good, like her.

My feet shift, tired from standing here so long. "So what are you saying?"

"I'm saying, it's okay to re-examine things. To bring Eric into the conversation, when that seems appropriate. Most of all, it's okay to admit to yourself that you're not okay with never having a biological child."

Looping her arm through mine once more, Lauren begins to walk, leading me back toward our friends, who are laughing one aisle over. "And it's okay to see if there are other options. If that's what you really want. If you don't, you can forget we had this conversation."

Acknowledging my own heart … that's a new one for me. I've known it for years, but denied it. Is it finally time to concede that what I want matters, like Alexis said several weeks ago?

As I allow my gaze to skitter along the edges of the baby store, I sigh. I just wish I knew what my mother would do. She'd be brave, that much I know.

But I don't know what the brave choice is anymore.

And that makes me more frightened than anything.

fifteen

. . .

WHEN I DON'T KNOW where else to go for answers, I come here.

The graveyard is quiet at dusk, cicadas singing a tune that's both peaceful and filled with mourning. Longing. How very accurate.

My family had a bench installed just beside Mom's headstone, so that whenever one of us feels like being close to her, we can come and sit, be comfortable. Tonight, the night before *Cinderella* opens, I find that there's nowhere else I'd rather be. Not even Eric has been able to help me snap out of the funk that's taken hold of me since last Friday night at the baby supply store. That plus tech week and dress rehearsals have made everything a blurry mess of emotions inside of me.

And when he pulled me aside tonight backstage, his eyes begged me to confide in him.

But how can I, when I don't know what I need to

say? What I want to say? There's so much warring in my heart. I want to be brave and good, like Mom, and I'm still fighting the instinct to run, to hide. To tell Eric I can't do this. Can't take away his choices. Even though we talked about it briefly, I know that there's a part of him that hasn't quite grasped what it means if he and I have a future together. What he'll be giving up.

Then, just when I'm resolved that this can't go on, Lauren's words come back. Hope comes back. *"It's okay to see if there are other options."*

And the cycle of hope, doubt, and fear begins all over again.

"Mom, I need some advice." The moon hides behind a grouping of dark clouds tonight, but its rays break through in sparse patches, enough to illuminate her name and epitaph: Linda Phillips. *Beloved wife and mother, nurturer of all, life giver, hope creator.*

She was indeed all of those things.

Am I? Have I lived up to my Dad's instruction to carry on Mom's legacy? Eric said I have. Is he right?

Headlights bounce off the stone as a lone car pulls into the graveyard, its tires popping along the gravel road. The vehicle stops a few feet away. I squint and recognize the brown Taurus. And when a tall man climbs out, my heart squeezes.

How did he know I was here? "Hi, Daddy."

My father approaches in his windbreaker and jeans, his steps favoring his left hip since he's due for a replacement in the next few months. "Hey, sweetheart." He sits down beside me and pats my knee. Before I can ask my question of him, he answers it. "Eric called, said you might be out here. Thought you might need to talk."

My chin trembles as I try to hold back my tears. "He did?"

"Mmm hmm. That boy sure does care about you."

"And I care about him." I haven't yet told my dad—or anyone else in my family—that Eric and I are dating now. To be honest, I wasn't sure how they'd take it. Is now a good time? Tucking my lip between my teeth, I lean my head against my dad's strong shoulder that has carried so much. "Daddy."

"I know, sugar. You two were made for each other."

My jaw drops and I pull back slightly to look at him. "How did you—"

"I recognize love when I see it." He's quiet as his gaze lands on Mom's grave. His mustache twitches. "And not that you need my approval, but you have it all the same."

At that, my shoulders relax. "Thanks, Dad."

"It's only a wonder it took you so long to realize it."

A long beat of time passes, the air so still it seems to hang in curtains around us. "I've known for a long time, actually."

Dad responds with a tiny grunt. "So what are you doing out here when you've got a good man you could be with? Did you have a fight?"

"No, nothing like that."

"Just nervous about tomorrow night, then?"

"Not nervous. Terrified."

He smiles. "Like mother like daughter, then."

My eyebrows lift. "What are you talking about? Mom was the bravest person I know."

"I agree, but there is no courage without fear."

Something pings in the back of my mind at hearing his words. "Mom used to say that."

"Every time she went on stage."

"Wait." I blink. "She had stage fright too?"

"Oh, it was terrible. She'd shake and sometimes even throw up—though she might murder me if she knew I was telling you this." Dad's arm slips around the back of the bench, around me, and he drums his fingers along the wood. "But, based on what Eric says, you're a beacon of beauty on that stage, and I can't wait to see you shine tomorrow night."

"Just pray I don't throw up *on* the stage."

He chuckles. "I hardly think that will happen. Just like Mom, you'll get out there and sing your heart out."

I fidget in my seat. "That's the thing, Dad. I'm not like Mom, even though I want to be."

He studies me in the starlight. Then, his brow lifts. "You're not talking about the show anymore, are you?"

Biting my lip, I shake my head.

"Is this about Eric?"

A nod. "There's something that I think he really wants. Something I can't give him." I inhale a shaky breath. "And I know the bravest thing I can do is sacrifice what *I* really want for the good of others. Mom did that over and over again."

"True. But a relationship is about dual sacrifice. I don't like that Eric is asking you to give up something you really want."

"Well … he's not."

"Ah." Dad strokes the ends of his mustache with his free hand. "Sweetie, even if you think you're doing the right thing, the brave thing—when you don't acknowledge what it is *you* want, you're holding back your heart from others. Despite the best of intentions, it's still one person dictating the course of things. And that isn't any kind of relationship at all."

Whoa. It's almost like he's echoing Lauren's words from Friday: *"If you guys end up together, then you should make a decision together."*

But I wasn't talking about whether to have kids. I was talking about whether to be with Eric in the first place. Then again, maybe it's all bound up in the same thing. "I'm just so terrified of losing again. And that's why … I don't want to have kids. I've got the gene, Daddy, and I can't stand the thought of possibly passing that on to children. Or of losing them. I barely survived losing Mom. I'd never survive *that*."

The confession, all I've been holding inside for so long, just spills out around me, soaking into the grass at my feet. Maybe speaking the words will somehow water the moment, help something to grow.

As if in response, the sky growls in the distance. A late summer storm is approaching.

"Ah, Shell-Bell." My dad's arms come completely around me, sheltering me from the world as he's always done.

I turn and cry into his shirt till it's soaked through. He smells like the spearmint gum he's constantly chewing. "Sorry, Daddy."

"There's nothing to be sorry for." He pulls back gently, holding my upper arms so I remain upright and we can look at each other. "Shelby, I understand your fear, but there's more than one way to lose out in life."

"What do you mean?" I reach into my purse and pull out a Kleenex package, then free a single tissue. A breeze cools the tears on my cheek, doing the tissue's work of drying them before I can swipe.

"In trying to protect yourself from future pain, you can easily lose your joy—and isn't finding joy what life is supposed to be about? Look at how your mom lived life to the fullest, even after her diagnosis."

He's right. She did.

I sniffle, nod. Droplets of rain begin to fall, misting our faces.

"This isn't about whether you will or won't have children. It's about taking one step at a time, trusting a power beyond yourself, and grappling for any joy this life will offer you."

There's that saying again—one step at a time.

He keeps going. "So ask yourself what you really want, stop holding yourself back, and sing your heart out—both figuratively and not."

Oh, Daddy.

He sighs. "And as for your mother, she was a wonderful woman. She was all the things you've said. Good, kind, brave." Dad's lips wobble then flatten into a frown as he inhales deeply, almost like he's trying not to cry. "I've never seen someone face death with such courage and peace as that woman did."

I grab his big, calloused hand and listen.

"But ... how do I say this? It's not unusual for us to remember our departed loved ones as better than they even were, to place them on a pedestal. Since they're gone now, they can't possibly fall off." Dad squeezes. "It's all right to want to live up to your mother's legacy, but just be sure you're not setting a false standard by assigning her the one characteristic she did not possess. Perfection."

My lips open, then close. I haven't made her perfect in my mind, have I?

Well. It's possible. I was so young when she died. And I've always been one to focus on the good if I can.

As we sit there beside the place where we laid Mom's body to rest, truth begins to sprout from the watered places in my soul one tiny blade at a time. The blades grow faster and faster, in time with the quickening rain.

I don't have to have all the answers right now.

Life isn't black and white. Mom wasn't all bravery or all fear. She was both. And I can be too.

If tomorrow night I completely fail—if I choke, or fall, or forget a line, or run off stage in tears—then I will not have failed. Not really. Failure would be not trying in the first place. Failure would be giving up. Failure would be running away.

I've been good at running away in the past, but that's okay. Because I can change. I don't have to be perfect, because Mom wasn't. Nobody is.

Oh my goodness, I *have* been holding myself to some impossible standard. Maybe I thought it would give my life meaning. Maybe I thought people would finally see me. But I realize … I've always been seen. By my friends. By my family.

And by the man I love more than music or air or life.

"Dad? I've gotta go."

"I suspected you might. Love you, baby girl."

I place a kiss on his scratchy cheek. "Love you more. Drive safe, okay?"

Then I'm sprinting down the road, climbing back into my car, and driving in the rain that's now coming in sheets, coming sideways, a renewed sense of purpose spurring me on. I head down the highway, my hands gripping the steering wheel as I consider exactly what to say.

And when I'm finally at a newly-familiar door on the outside ground floor of an apartment complex, I shiver and knock.

The door creaks open and Eric's face first lights up then darkens with concern. "Shelbs? You okay? Get in here."

"You know," I say, my lips chattering. "I always thought it would be really romantic to be kissed in the rain."

"Is that so?" That lazy smile of his that I love so much clicks into place. He takes a step out, joining me in the deluge. His hands slide into mine as he leans in, pressing his mouth close to my ear. "And is it also romantic to catch a cold the night before a big performance?"

I laugh and shrug. "I don't really care about that."

"Really? Seems like caring has eaten you up all week."

Letting go of his hands, I take his Padres hat and place it on my head.

And he doesn't even bat an eye. "That looks good on you. Right at home."

The water pours from the sky and plays a symphony on the pavement. I'm cold but have no wish to go inside, because there's seriously something magical about this music.

I grab hold of the sides of his T-shirt and pull him toward me.

Eric comes willingly, angling his face just above mine. "What's gotten into you? Not that I'm complaining." Water drips from his hair, his eyelashes, his nose. It's a sexy look on him.

"Just finally going for exactly what I want. And that's you, Eric. It's always been you." Throwing away a lifetime with this man—if that's where this leads—because of a false savior complex would be pure foolishness when there's so much joy, so much laughter, to be had.

"I'm glad to hear it. This week you've seemed … well, like you might be changing your mind."

"I'll never change my mind." Then I realize how that sounds—like I'm telling him I'm his, forever. Then again, I kind of am. Still, we've technically only dated for thirteen days and I don't want the intensity of my affection to scare him off. "I didn't mean for that to sound like—"

"I'll never change mine either." As usual, Eric knows what I'm going to say. He tucks my hair behind my ear.

"You're it for me, Shelby Phillips. If I don't marry *you*, I'm going to die a sad and lonely man."

"Eric," I chuckle. My insides squeeze.

But he's not joking. Taking my face gently between his hands, he gets nose to nose with me. "This is either way too early to say this or way too late since it's seventeen years in the making, but I love you, Shelby Phillips. I love you and I always will."

I start to cry again, this time happy tears that mingle with the rain. "I know that I've been so wishy-washy lately about our future, about the whole having kids or not having kids thing." My chest is heaving. "But I've never been wishy washy about how much I love you. That's always been the case, and it will be forever. And I promise … I'm open to whatever our future brings. Whatever discussions we need to have, whatever trials we need to face. I just want to face them head-on with you. And only you."

"You have no idea how happy I am to hear you say that."

"Well." I smile. "I'm happy that you're happy."

"The happiest." Then he kisses me and my heart is singin' in the rain.

Eric Moody is the culmination of all my wildest dreams—even the ones I didn't have the courage to dream for myself.

And I'm not letting go for anything.

epilogue

. . .

Alexis

I AM OFFICIALLY A NINTH WHEEL.

Well, fine, currently there are only eight of us leaving our seats during intermission inside the Redmont Ridge Elementary fine arts building, but that's because Shelby is still backstage after an amazing first act. Even Topher flew out for a long weekend to see the performance. More like, he couldn't stand to be away from Lauren for longer than a week. Gag me. But I'm happy for Lauren. Really.

I'm happy for all of them. Evie, Kayla, and Shelby too. The fact that they found good guys in a sea of pigs —well, that's nothing short of miraculous, really. And I knew it would happen eventually. I started alone in my house. And soon, once Lauren and Shelby inevitably get married and move out, I'll be alone again.

Maybe it's time for me to get a cat. Or maybe I can convince Kennedy to leave her terrible boyfriend and come live here with me. Or maybe I really can handle the remainder of the mortgage all by myself. Getting the Charles account—and the bonus that goes with it—sure would help.

I should find out on Monday if it went to me or good-for-nothing-but-looking-pretty Dax Nyhart. Despite all my best efforts, my boss—his uncle—gave him the McMahon project. And I honestly wouldn't be surprised if it happens again.

"Who knew she could sing so well?" Evie says as Connor opens the door from the auditorium out into the lobby. The air conditioning tosses her brown bangs back and she holds onto her stomach as if it's going to blow away too.

"She's amazing, isn't she?" Eric switches the bouquet of purple flowers and bag of Skittles from one hand to the other and wipes a bit of sweat from his forehead. Don't know why he's the one who looks nervous when it's Shelby performing. Maybe it has something to do with the fact I'm fairly certain he's going to propose tonight after the show. If not then, soon.

And then, there will be one. Two, if I get that cat.

"I loved how she laughed at herself when she forgot a few lines of her song," Lauren says.

"I know she was nervous about that happening." I nod. "But she just shrugged and kept on going." And I'm proud of her for that. She's come a really long way as far as self-confidence goes. And she deserves her minutes in the spotlight. Shelby is one amazing human and I'm lucky to call her a friend. (But if you ever tell her I said that, I'll hunt you down, *capisce*?)

"Aw, look." Kayla points across the crowded lobby

at a loud group of people. Several adults are talking loudly, and kids are running around playing tag. "Shelby's family is all here."

Yep, the entire brood—from her parents to all of her siblings to every single niece and nephew, including the babies—are gathered around the refreshments table. I spot Deb, her older sister, who has a good head on her shoulders.

Josh adjusts his hipster glasses. "I'm going to hit the restroom before the second act hits."

"Oh yes, this baby's been sitting on my bladder the entire show. Size of a bell pepper, my rear. This thing has got to be as big as a pumpkin at least."

Her husband strokes her belly with his thumb. "You be nice to your mom, okay, Baby Rey?"

"Aw." Kayla reaches around and pinches his butt. "You're so hot when you use your dad voice, Solo."

For the love … "Excuse me while I go throw up." I hightail it through the crowd, dodging all the faceless people I don't know until I get to Deb. "Hey."

She turns to me, grins. "Hey, Alexis. Love the hair tonight."

I toss my ponytail over my shoulder. "Thanks." Last night I died my hair blue in support of Shelby—it's now the color of Cinderella's dress. "Felt like time for a change."

Her eyes sparkle. "Because a week is such a long time."

Dying my hair started in high school as a way to stand out in a sea of lemmings. It was the only individuality allowed at my East Coast boarding school, and I was relegated to colors that looked "natural." So when I graduated and moved out to California to be near my half-sister, Kennedy, I fully embraced the rebellion, however retroactive it may be.

I shrug. "Carpe diem, right? Hey, Shelby's doing great."

"She really is, isn't she?" Deb's eyes shine. "She reminds me of Mom up there."

"You should tell her that."

"I will."

Just then, one of Deb's children snags her attention for the moment, so I turn to the refreshments table and peruse the offerings there. Cookies, brownies, individual carrot cakes, donuts. Everything is ridiculously expensive, but according to a sign at the end of the table, all the proceeds go to the arts department, so I reach into my mini backpack purse for my wallet and pull out a five.

Moving to the other side of the table, I spy oatmeal pies—and freeze. My entire body goes numb. I haven't had one of those since my dad's funeral.

Since the week I found out—

"Oh, you don't want to eat one of those, hon."

My focus is shattered by an uppity voice to my left. I swivel to find a stick-thin blonde wearing a little black dress as if we were at the opera instead of a children's play. Her hair is perfectly highlighted and smoothly styled, and her heeled pumps give her an extra three inches.

"Excuse me?"

She leans in like we're besties and she's got a secret

to tell me. "Those oatmeal pies are, like, two hundred calories."

I place my hand against my chest and gasp. "No!"

Apparently she believes I'm truly stunned by her revelation, because she nods fiercely, eyes wide. "Can you believe it? That's, like, one-third of my daily caloric intake."

Okay, now I really do gasp. This chick subsists on six hundred calories a day? (Either that or she can't do math. It could really go either way.) "That's inhumane." And I mean it.

"I know. They should have asked *me* to run the table. I'd have stocked it full of yummy treats, like kale chips and ooo—I have the most delicious recipe for bran muffins." At my skeptical look, she pats my arm like I'm six years old. "Shocking, right?"

"I'm speechless." Moreover, I'm so done with this conversation. I snag an oatmeal pie and cackle on the inside at her wide eyes and flopping lips. "Well, I'd better go pay for this. I'll eat it for both of us."

Then I lift it in salute and her perfectly proportioned face contorts. Thanks to my lovely prep school education, I can see what's coming—a thinly veiled insult of some kind. But because I've become an expert in avoidance, I pivot a one-eighty to escape it just in time.

And run smack into a hard chest.

Correction: My oatmeal pie runs smack into a hard chest.

"Aw, man." I'm gonna have to pay for that AND apologize to some random guy for my clumsiness. "I'm so s—"

"Rainbow Brite? What are you doing here?"

Oh no. No, no, noooooo. That grating voice—filled with self-amusement and taunting me with that terrible nickname—cannot be invading my space right now. It's supposed to be the weekend. My one reprieve from him.

I squeeze my eyes shut, count to five, then reopen one of them. Peek up.

Crap on a stick.

There stands Dax Nyhart, my nemesis, with his perfectly styled deep brown hair, olive complexion, and laughing green eyes. He's still wearing the same red polo and jeans he wore into the office today and, darn him, he still smells like cinnamon warmed over.

The only thing that gives me a wink of satisfaction is the cream-filled pastry smashed on his shirt.

Before I can respond to his question, Stick-Thin Opera Barbie rushes over. "Oh my goodness! Are you okay, Daxy?"

Daxy?

"I'm fine, Lilith." He glances down at his shirt then leans toward the table to snatch a napkin. "Lilith, this is my co-worker, Alexis. Alexis, this is my fiancée, Lilith."

Fiancée? I've never heard him mention a fiancée. Then again, I try to ignore all things Dax Nyhart if possible.

Lilith and Daxy. What a pair.

"Oh." Lilith teeters, and hangs on Dax's arm. "Nice to meet you."

"Yeah, sure. Same." I'm so over this. I need to get inside the theater. Since my fingers are filled with smushed pie, I reach for a napkin too, only to see that Dax has taken the last one. Grrr.

He sees my scowl, grins, and hands me his crumpled, used napkin.

I am seriously considering using the rest of his shirt instead—teach him a lesson in chivalry—but Lilith's eagle eyes are on me and I'm not willing to risk her attempts to fight me if I go near her man again. Those spiked red fingernails look downright dangerous.

"Well, if you'll excuse me, I need to go wash my hands and find my seat again. My roommate is playing the lead." Take that, Lilac. Or was it Tulip?

"My niece is the queen and she's, like, so adorable." Dax's fiancée doesn't remove her beady eyes from me.

"Cool." I maneuver around the couple. *Bye, crazy lady.*

"Is that the girl you beat out for the Charles account?" she whispers loud enough for the whole state of California to hear.

And I know she's baiting me but I can't help but whip back around. "What?"

Dax has the decency to narrow his eyes at his fiancée before turning to me with a tight smile. "Uh, yeah. Nate just told me this afternoon."

Nate. Ha. "You're not fooling anyone by leaving off the 'uncle' in his name." My lip curls. "We all know why you keep landing the best accounts."

"How dare you? Daxy got the account fair and square." Lilith practically purrs as she pets his arm. "He's the best and deserves the best."

The best, huh? I narrow my eyes. "We'll see about that."

How am I ever going to get past the office politics that are currently in play to prove that he's not in fact the best? I've been trying for at least a year with no success. So yeah. No idea.

All I *do* know?

Dax Nyhart has got to go. Out of our office—and out of my life.

Thanks for hanging with Eric, Shelby, and the rest of the gang! If you enjoyed your visit with them, would you consider leaving a review?

And if you, like me, love a good enemies-to-lovers story, then you'll definitely want to **check out Alexis's book**, *Engaging the Office Enemy*.

Want a little more of Shelby and Eric's happily ever after? Download the *Belonging With Her Best Friend* Bonus Epilogue at kristincanary.com/bestfriend.

sneak peek

Engaging the Office Enemy

If I had a choice between poking my own eye out with a fork and staying in this meeting, well, pass the cutlery, please.

Alas, I do not have a choice. So like a good little employee, I sit here and take the garbage that Adolf Jones—the CEO of the one-man company that is Jonesing for Coffee—spews in my direction.

Who names their kid Adolf anyway? I almost feel sorry enough for the man to forgive him for his rude treatment of me, but his snarled lip and meaty finger pointed my way are enough to snuff that small flicker of sympathy.

Leaning back in my office chair, I tug the end of my long purple braid around to my lap while Adolf rails on about the many ways in which I have failed him as a graphic designer and brand manager (the latter of which I never wanted to be anyway). The fifty-something's got a super bushy Fu Manchu mustache draped over his lip like a limp fuzzy snake, and he strokes and rolls it like it's a weapon he's sharpening for later use. His rotund stomach is about to burst the buttons on his crisp khaki-colored business suit as he inhales for another volley. I find myself hoping it happens—something, anything, to break up this little hate fest.

But it doesn't, and he keeps on going. Looks like it's up to me to draw this meeting to a close. What's new? "Mr. Jones, I'm so sorry you feel that I haven't provided you with the results you've needed," I interject in the most neutral—and bored—tone I can manage.

Could I have added in a little more charm? More simpering? Made myself "less than" just to give someone else an inflated sense of self-importance? Probably, and that would make my boss, Nate Birmingham, super happy. But you know what? I refuse to suck up to people, especially ones who don't deserve it. I speak the truth and nothing but the truth—though maybe not all the truth. And yeah, maybe it gets me into trouble sometimes.

Maybe it's also the reason I only have a few friends, a close-knit group I've been lucky enough to call mine even though it makes me slightly terrified that one day they'll leave me too. A few already have.

And yes, I realize that getting married and having babies isn't really *leaving* me (I feel eye-rollingly dramatic even thinking it), but the effect is the same. Once my roommates Lauren and Shelby get married next year, I'm going to be Alexis Matkin, *that one crazy cat lady over on Sandy Street.*

Just need the cat and I'll be set.

"I suppose I shouldn't be surprised." Mr. Jones leans forward, and one of the buttons looks close to coming unthreaded. *Come on, baby. Pop!* "You take little care with your own appearance. I don't know why I would think you'd take care with my brand."

Whoa, now. I literally bite my tongue from responding in kind, because I don't stoop to personal insults. People have their own styles—I'm cool with that. I just wish he hadn't brought mine into it. No, I don't wear the adorable skirts and blouses my friend Shelby-the-kindergarten-teacher does, or the gym-chic clothes Lauren wears, or the hot-mama dresses Kayla does, or Evie's librarian-esque sweaters. But I happen to like the jeans and vintage Thor T-shirt I'm currently rocking along with a pair of Birkenstocks (yes, it's October, but sandals are a year-round affair in California). They're comfortable and every day is casual Friday around here, after all. Even Thursdays, like today.

Don't get me wrong. I actually appreciate Mr. Jones's authenticity in this moment. At least he isn't pretending like he's satisfied with my work or beating around the bush. He's being straightforward. But he's also being super rude, and ain't nobody got time for that.

With an abrupt push away from the desk, I stand. "Sorry, I have another meeting." And I do—it's called lunch with me, myself, and I.

His mouth stops moving, and the last syllable teeters on the edge of his lips. "Yes, well." Lumbering to his feet, he looks around my office and blinks. "It's very hard to focus in here, isn't it, Ms. Matkin?"

"I've told you. It's Alexis." If I could scrub all

familial association with my father, I would. But changing my last name would be scrubbing my association with Kennedy too, and that's never happening. Still. Formality is not my thing. "And I happen to focus quite well in here."

The ninety square feet of space I've been allotted at Birmingham & Co. Media—a small marketing firm in San Diego—is my sanctuary from the boring grays and cool blues of the rest of the office. Every time I see the vibrant green walls with abstract yellow and pink artwork, it energizes me, fuels my creativity. The effect is helped along by the large window to my right that boasts a view of the park down below, verdant and lush and not soul-killing in the least.

Staring out that window—imagining myself there, swinging like a child, hair blowing freely in the wind— is how I survive the monotonous parts of my job.

And the times where I'm being yelled at too, which seem to be occurring more and more frequently, all because my boss keeps handing over the good accounts to his nephew, the obnoxiously charming—and completely fake—Dax Nyhart, leaving me with the left-over scraps.

Mr. Jones clears his throat again, a sound that's a mix between a frog croaking and a heavy truck driving over gravel. "I do hope I can expect better results in the future. My company's products are of utmost quality and deserve to be recognized as the exciting commodity they are."

I cough, managing to suppress a comment about how coffee filters are the least exciting product known to man (especially since I can't stand the disgusting black brew so many people call the elixir of life). See? My boss's lecture on being nice to the clients has had some effect, whatever he may think.

"As always, I'll do my best." Without another word, I usher Mr. Jones out of my office and begin the short walk toward the clear front door. The hallway is lined with motivational posters, and just like every time I pass, I edit them in my brain. (For example, the one that says "If you never try, you'll never know" gets "how terrible you are" added to the end. Why must we pretend that everyone who tries something will be amazing at it?)

It doesn't take long to reach the main office, where there are a cluster of cubicles and about four salesmen whose names I can't distinguish because, despite their varying job titles, they're essentially carbon copies of one another. Same designer hairstyles. Same over-muscled chests they clearly spend hours in the gym achieving. Same crass jokes. Reminds me of Dr. Strange cloning himself in one of my favorite movies, *Avengers: Infinity Wars*—except instead of fighting the evil dude Thanos, they're battling good things like individuality and authenticity.

Between them, the receptionist (Gina), our boss (Nate), tech guru (Penelope), and the other two designers (Dax and Rupert), it's a small office, with HR and accounting being farmed out to another company. There are exactly zero people here whose company I enjoy, unless you count Juan, the janitor who has been known to share his menudo with me on the nights I work past midnight (which has grown more often as of late).

As Adolf shuffles out the door, Gina waves a friendly goodbye to him from behind her plain black desk, then looks at me sideways and writes something in her notebook. It couldn't be more obvious that the forty-something mom of three doesn't like me and believes it her sole mission to report on the misdeeds of everyone in the office. With her high tight bun and prim black suit jacket, she's the exact opposite of my ever-changing hair colors and more casual style. She's only got about a decade on me, but acts like her maturity and wisdom are divine gifts to this office.

"Gina." I nod at her with I-know-what-you're-doing eyes.

Her lips draw into a straight line. "Alexis."

My stomach gurgles and I press a fist against it. Time to lock myself in my office and count down the minutes until six p.m. At least all of my client meetings are done for the day and I can spend the afternoon creating, lose myself for a little bit. I can also take a few minutes to text Kennedy back about her latest boyfriend crisis. Maybe I can convince her to finally leave the worthless guy she's with and move down here from San Francisco. After all, within the next year, there will be plenty of room in la Casa de Alexis.

The as-yet-nonexistent cat will only take up a tiny bit of space, I imagine. Ooo, unless I decide to go for more than one. That would really seal the cat-lady reputation.

Heading to the break room, I grab my lunch out of the fridge and bring it back to my office. My bright blue tumbler is empty, so I trudge back past the Drs. Strange and to the other side of Gina's desk, where the water cooler sits. Tipping my cup under the spout, I turn on the spigot and inhale a breath as a stream of water flows into my cup.

Maybe it's the waxy plants in the corner, the white walls, the air that's always tinged with a smell that's strangely reminiscent of the powdered orange Tang they served at my boarding school in place of real orange juice, but something about this place has always made me feel a little bit caged in. Claustrophobic.

I studied graphic design in college and really do love it. What I don't love is creating art for other people, especially since working here requires me to wear the hats of both designer and marketing guru-slash-brand manager. So are there days I dream about leaving Birmingham & Co., finding a job that's less about marketing and more about the art? Or at the very least, something that doesn't bear the burden of someone's entire brand?

Sure. But the idea of going out on my own, the instability of it all … well, remember what I said about preferring to poke my eye out? There's not really a choice in this either.

Because this job pays the bills, allowing me to be independent—and that's the most important thing. In fact, I'm within reach of finally paying off the mortgage on the partially-owned house my aunt left me nine years ago when she decided to move to Europe on a whim. If only I could get rid of a certain someone who keeps taking all the good clients because he's related to the boss—

"Thank you for your time today, Ms. Longenecker. It's been an absolute pleasure." A voice floats down the hallway, growing louder by the second.

Speak of the devil.

The tall, smug, broad-shouldered devil with a capital D.

Dax Nyhart comes strolling down the hallway with our top-billing client, Aretha Longenecker of Longenecker Homes. Besides being a very genteel sort of person, and genuine to boot, her company sells inspired, recycled products for the home that are legit doing a ton to save the environment. Hers is the mecca of accounts, and who do you think landed it without so much as an audition?

If you guessed the infuriating nephew of the boss, you'd be correct.

"The pleasure is all mine, Dax." Aretha extends her sleek brown hand and shakes my mortal enemy's, her face all serenity and smiles. She's a tiny thing, but that doesn't fool anyone around here. The woman is a brilliant powerhouse, and you wouldn't find *her* yelling at someone she's hired or insulting their clothing as petty revenge for lackluster results her own product was responsible for.

There are three of us who manage accounts—Dax, me, and Rupert, who is nearing retirement and couldn't care less about what clients he gets so long as he can do the least amount of work possible—and who do you think is the one getting all the best clients?

Not me, that's for sure, even though my work is definitely superior. Not to toot my own horn, but I give credit where it's due.

And it's NOT due to Dax.

Just because he's objectively handsome—with his long torso, tan skin, brown hair that's as carefully controlled as his temper, and that crooked smile he throws around like candy—doesn't mean he's talented at anything other than schmoozing.

Water hits my bare toes and I yelp when I realize my tumbler is overflowing. Cursing under my breath, I stop the spigot, drink a bit of excess from the top of the cup, slip the lid back on, and dry my fingers on my jeans.

While I'm cleaning myself up, the front door opens and Aretha's heels on the tile floor punctuate her exit. I watch her clip down the hallway and press the elevator button. Too bad I can't join her, but I've got about three and a half more hours until freedom will be mine.

Temporary freedom, until tomorrow arrives—but I'll take what I can get. Besides, tonight should be fun. I get to hang out with my friends.

"Man, I love working with Aretha." Dax's grating voice materializes beside me, and his snickerdoodles-right-out-of-the-oven scent breezes under my nose. "So intelligent. So kind." He pauses. "So *not* named after ruthless dictators."

I tilt my gaze upward and narrow it into a glare despite the way his arresting, amused eyes lock onto mine. His irises are a mixture of green and gold that I can't help but find fascinating—purely from an artistic point of view, of course. "I don't know what you mean."

My tone is forcefully even. "Adolf is amazing. He and I are best buds."

"I completely believe it." He grins at me in that lazy way of his. "You probably won him over with your cheery personality." Dax grabs a Hershey's kiss from the bowl on Gina's desk. As he unwraps the foil packaging, he doesn't seem to notice that our very married receptionist watches him with the end of her pen in her mouth, clicking it against her teeth, a far-away look in her eye.

Seriously, why is every female so enamored with this guy? Don't they know he's engaged, anyway? I met his fiancée a few months ago at my friend Shelby's performance of *Cinderella*. A real winner, she was—one of those bone-thin women who never thinks she's skinny enough, a perfect duplicate of all the girls I encountered at the Connecticut boarding school my mom enrolled me in after my father died and his big secret came out.

Moving to California after graduation five years later to be closer to my half-sister was the best decision I ever made, even if it led me to be in the same office as the obnoxious man in front of me.

I puff out my chest just a little. "Talent should matter more than personality. And there's nothing wrong with mine."

Gina snorts and I toss her a death glare.

"Never said there was, Rainbow Brite."

Gritting my teeth against the ridiculous nickname Dax gave me on his second week of working here, I arch my eyebrows. "We can't all be pompous suck-ups, now can we?"

He leans in close, and my body rebels against my better judgment as a shiver works its way up my spine. "No, but I can teach you some tricks to succeed, if you'd like."

He thinks his nearness is intimidating, but it's not. I step closer, so he'll know *I know* what he's trying to pull. "How's that, when all you really need to do well at this company is some good old-fashioned nepotism?"

And here's how I know he's a complete faker, because that comment would bother any mere mortal, especially a man (because men in general are nothing if not proud creatures who like to go around beating their chests and declaring their own prowess). Yet Dax stands there, looking at me, still smiling and completely nonplussed. "Admit it, RB. I just do my job really, really well."

"Hmm, I don't recall flirting and brownnosing being part of our job description."

"It's called improvising. You should try it."

"One of us has to take this job seriously."

"Some might say too seriously." He tilts his chin. "You work too hard, RB."

Is he for real? "And you don't work hard enough."

Someone clears a throat nearby and I startle, pulling my gaze momentarily from Dax to the bank of eyes in the cubicles across the room. And now the Drs. Strange are flashing identical grins at each other and us, a murmur building between them. I roll my eyes and start moving toward the hallway.

But a hand on my upper arm stops me.

Dax's touch burns into my skin and I shake him off. "What?"

He's close, again, and I lick my teeth to keep from noticing the way the purple polo shirt he's wearing pulls taut against his shoulders, makes his eyes pop. "Admit it, RB. I make this job more fun."

Huffing out a caustic laugh, I shake my head. "That's exactly the type of thing I'd expect you to say. You really don't have a clue, do you?"

"A clue about how much you'd miss me if we didn't work together anymore?"

What a strange thing to say, but then again, I'm used to the most unusual drivel coming from his mouth.

There's only one way to deal with prideful jerks like him. Throw them off their game. So I curve my lips into a sweet smile and look at him with what I hope present as wide, adoring eyes. "Dax."

For a moment, something flickers in his eyes—like he doesn't quite know what to make of me, like the mask he always keeps so securely in place slips just a little. Well, good. Fakers are the worst and he's as fake as they come.

"Yeah?"

"I would miss you"—my words are pure honey in the air—"about as much as Captain America misses Red Skull."

"Huh?"

Oh my goodness. Does this man seriously not know his Marvel trivia? "I can't even with you." Once again, I start toward the hallway.

"Wait, RB." A pause. "Alexis—"

I turn to tell him to leave me alone, but he's closer than I think and I ram into his solid chest, water sloshing out the straw hole in my lid onto both of our shirts. He throws a hand on my hip to steady me.

And I feel that grip all the way to my toes, its zap as sudden and unwanted as lightning. Our gazes collide and I'm close enough to see the slight dusting of stubble on his jaw. He opens his mouth to speak—

"Yo, Nyhart!"

One of the Drs. Strange shouts Dax's name and he blinks, then takes a step back from me. He glances up just in time to see a football sailing through the air. One-handed and calm, he reaches up and grabs it—to a wild round of cheers—then hauls back and returns it to the dude. He shoots the guy a thumbs-up and the mask is fully intact once more.

Clearly, it's not just women who are obsessed with Dax Nyhart. Everyone else falls so easily for his lies and manipulation, believing he's really a good guy who is genuinely happy all the time.

But no one is happy all the time. Everyone is hiding something. And I don't trust the ones who pretend they aren't. I've done that before—twice. First with my dad. Then with Corbin. And twice, it's come back to bite me.

I refuse to be the fool who falls for it a third time.

So while Dax is preoccupied, I retreat to my office, lock the door, and eat my lunch alone.

Just the way I like it.

books by kristin canary

California Dreamin' Series

Enamoring Her Amnesic Ex (prequel)

Loving the Ladies' Man

Desiring His Dating Coach

Saving the Secret Prince

Belonging With Her Best Friend

Engaging the Office Enemy

Needing the Next-Door Neighbor

Hallmark Beach Series

Beachside Kisses With My Bodyguard

about the author

Kristin is a wife and boy mom who functions best on peach tea and cookie dough ice cream. A desert dweller, she always has her eye on the next trip to a beach somewhere—and if she can't travel there in person, then you'd better believe she's going to write about it. Kristin is never fully satisfied with a movie, TV show, or book without a hefty dose of romance in it, and she's grateful to be living a true-life love story with her own crazy little family. Connect with her at KristinCanary.com.

facebook.com/kristincanary

instagram.com/kristincanaryauthor